THE FOSTER CHILDREN OF TIME

Book I of
Temporal Affairs

Robert Schell

The Foster Children of Time: Book I of Temporal Affairs by Robert Schell
© 2013 (as Time Station: Book I of The Foster Children of Time)

Published by Robert Schell
Doebird Publishing
McAllen, Texas

http://pcqgod.wix.com/robert-schell

Cover art and design © 2013 by Travis Klein – tibbodeaux.wix.com/ allterraingraphics

ISBN number: 978-0-9899911-0-0

Library of Congress Control Number: 2013918955

First Edition
Printed in the United States of America

For Ann Marie.
Hope it was worth the wait.

"Thou foster child of silence and slow time,
Sylvan historian, who canst thus express
A flowery tale more sweetly than our rhyme"

John Keats "Ode on a Grecian Urn" (1819)

Tony Marco was born in the year 2001, which was, according to the Gregorian calendar, the first year of the 21st Century and also the first year of the Third Millennium A.D. The Gregorian calendar was named after Pope Gregory XIII, who implemented it by having Friday, October 15 immediately follow Thursday, October 4 in the year 1582 A.D., causing a good portion of Europe to essentially skip forward ten days in time.

May 11, 2001, the date of Tony Marco's birth, was the day that humorist Douglas Adams, who wrote *The Hitchhiker's Guide to the Galaxy*, passed away, and was also the 181st anniversary of the launch of the H.M.S. Beagle from the Woolwich Dockyard on the river Thames in England. Historians looking back at the early 21st Century (when time was still thought of as a linear phenomenon) note the following events: the respective orbits of Mars and Earth carried both worlds to their closest approach in 60,000 years, culminating on August 27, 2003; in French Guiana, the birth of a polydactyl man who would be considered a prophet in a major world religion centuries later; in the Rapti Anchal of Nepal, the first documented appearance of a pituitary gland mutation in poultry.

Important events of the Temporal Summoning also occurred in the dawning years of the Third Millennium A.D., although this was unknown to most people at the time. Tony Marco would play a significant part in the events of the Temporal Summoning and the dissolution of the First Time Confederation, but that would come later in his life, after his first visit to the Khronos-Solarin Time Station.

Tony Marco was born one month prematurely to Elena Marco, a case-worker for Child Protective Services and one-time junior high 800 meter track champion of Corpus Christi, Texas, while she was riding a bus. Elena's husband Rudy, a musician, amateur painter, and self-described recovering football addict, was at her side and assisted, as best as he could, in the birthing process. Afterwards, Rudy resisted Elena's suggestions that they have more children, and so Tony grew up as an only child. While a toddler, Tony developed an odd fascination with shirt and coat buttons. When no one was about, Tony would open the closet door in his parents' room and run his hands over the false wood-grain buttons of Rudy's old tan blazer. This pastime was soon to be replaced by a borderline obsession with the various beetles, pill bugs, snails, and caterpillars to be found scurrying about the Marco family's backyard. When Tony had just turned three, he amazed everyone present at his cousin Sara's confirmation by climbing on top of a pew and announcing at the top of his lungs, "I like turtles and dinosaurs!" and then proceeding to sing a verse of Ricky Martin's "Livin la Vida Loca" before Elena pulled him down.

Tony was a curious boy, and would often drive Elena to near distraction by asking her questions that she did not know the answers to. These are some of the questions that Tony asked Elena:

"Do birds have favorite songs?"

"If a person never stopped growing, how tall would they get if they lived to 100?"

"Could you drive a car to the Moon if someone built a road up to it?"

"How high could a kangaroo on a trampoline jump?"

"Will Dad be home for my birthday this year?"

One day at a yard sale Elena came across a set of books called The Young American Scholar's Science and History Encyclopedia. She purchased the entire set for twenty dollars and gifted it to Tony, who was delighted. He spent many hours in his room (when he was not running about the neighborhood with his friends) reading through random articles in the encyclopedia. Tony was most often drawn to the second volume, which began with Alaric the Visigoth and ended with the rise and fall of the Aztec Empire.

❧◉◉☙

The spider web was at least five feet in length, tenuously suspended between the twin transplanted Australian bottle trees standing in the front yard of the Marco home. The web was a fragile, ethereal thing that glistened in the sun and seemingly vanished the next second. Tony Marco stared in wonder, marveling at the tenacity of the spider that spun it.

"Tony," Elena called from the door, "Invite Caroline to Arthur's party!"

"If I see her, mom," he yelled back as he took one last look at the web, its gossamer strands already threatening to unravel in the morning breeze. Tony spied his father serenely polishing the hood of his vintage 1972 Camaro in the garage.

"Dad! The Cowboys won last night!"

"I don't want to hear about it!" Rudy grumbled without turning from his work.

Tony chuckled and walked up to the corner where Carson and Martin were already waiting for the school bus. It was a mild late September day. Dragonflies buzzed crossways over newly mown lawns and whiptail lizards darted over sidewalks, seeming to hardly touch the ground at all. The hot roaring south Texas summer winds had finally ceased their relentless sweep over the dry land, and for the first time there was just the slightest hint of autumn in the air. Tony caught a hint of the sea in the breeze.

"Tony, my man!" called out Carson.

"Hey," said Tony, exchanging the usual ritualistic hand clasps with his friends.

"I hear there's a righteous shindig going down at Casa Marco tonight."

Carson was second generation American Vietnamese, tall and of almost fragile thinness. As usual he stood with his head cocked back

3

as if sniffing something offensive right in front of him, but Tony was accustomed to his friend's off-putting mannerisms.

"Yeah, my cousin Arthur's going away party. He's not deploying for another week, so I don't know why it has to be tonight."

Tony shrugged.

"Is that emo friend of yours invited?"

Carson was obviously trying to strike a nerve.

"Caroline's not emo," replied Tony evenly, refusing to be baited. "Anyway, we just used to hang out years ago when our parents visited. I don't even really talk to her much anymore."

"Do you believe this guy, Martin?"

Carson grinned as if in possession of secret knowledge.

"Or maybe you've already invited Mandy? Three's a crowd, they say."

"I wish. I don't think Mandy has spoken to me since first grade. And that was just to tell me not to sit next to her."

"That's too bad, son. Mandy is several kinds of new and unclassified fine."

"Forget that party, homes," said Martin, breaking into the conversation, "Tonight it's Nuevo Laredo. Food, dance... ladies!"

Martin was an athletically built young man, a year older than Carson and Tony. For a year after moving into the neighborhood he had callously bullied them. After Tony and Carson staged an elaborate prank at school involving various lab chemicals, popcorn, and a taxidermied panther mascot (which resulted in Carson's eyebrows being singed and the dispatch of three fire response units), Martin abruptly accepted both as friends as if there had never been any bad blood.

"Oh no!" protested Tony, "I don't want to be the wheelman for your crime spree in Mexico! I just got my learner's permit."

Martin laughed dismissively, brushing a wind-blown strand of hair out of his face.

"*Tranquilo*, man. You don't even have to drive. Silvan has his license already."

Tony regarded Martin with some suspicion.

"Seriously?"

"Is the Pope bald?"

"I don't know. He's always wearing that little hat."

"Translation: time to man up," said Carson, adding his weight to the tug-of-war of wills.

The school bus pulled up to the curb and they boarded. They claimed their usual seat in back. Carson yanked a window down as the bus rumbled into traffic.

Tony mulled Martin's proposition over. He wasn't terribly excited about the prospect of attending his cousin Arthur's party. It wasn't that he had any personal issues with Arthur; he had a comfortable enough relationship with his cousin, although they weren't especially close. But every family gathering seem to devolve into the same routine of slideshows, half-burned barbeque chicken, Grandpa Ray telling overly-familiar stories about his time overseas in Scotland, and a procession of fawning Aunts pinching his cheek.

"Okay, I'll do it," Tony finally answered, simultaneously feeling a sense of self-accomplishment at having made such a momentous decision, and a fair amount of dread upon considering what potential disaster he might be getting himself into.

The bus deposited them in front of Diaz High School. Tony parted with Carson and Martin outside the gym, where they both had first period P.E. and continued indoors to his English Literature class.

Mrs. Livingston stood as if at attention at the door of her class, clutching a clipboard. She waved at Tony.

"Do you have a minute? I liked your paper on early exploration in Texas. With a bit of spit and polish, I think we could enter it in the Carancahua History Association's competition this year. Are you interested?"

"Um...possibly?"

"Well, I'm sure you must have a busy schedule. I was a teenager once. Not that long ago, I'd like to think."

"I've been meaning to ask, how *did* people even survive back in the dark ages of dial-up?"

"Oh, you rascal. Run along now. We can discuss this later after third period."

Tony continued down the hall to his locker, lost in thoughts of the road trip to Nuevo Laredo.

"Hi, Tony."

Startled out of his reverie, Tony noticed Mandy slinking by.

"Hey there, Mandy!" he replied, trying to sound as nonchalant as possible. He let out a low whistle, watching Mandy glide into Literature class, books clutched to her chest. Tony grabbed his texts and turned to follow. Caroline was standing directly in his path. She took her earbuds out and approached slowly.

"Hello," she said, as if asking a question.

"Hello, Caroline."

Silence.

"So what's up with you, Tony? Anything interesting going on with you?"

"Huh? No. Not really. Just...same old."

"You know we really haven't talked in a long..."

The first period bell rang.

"Sorry, Caroline. We can catch up some other time, okay?"

"Alright. Sure."

Tony walked in. There was an unoccupied desk next to Mandy's in the front row and Tony moved to claim it, but Caroline plopped down in it. Sighing, Tony settled for the desk next to Caroline's.

"Okay, people," said Miss Sandoval in a no-nonsense tone, "Please take the first twenty minutes of class to read the poems by John Keats starting on page 134 of your texts."

Tony glanced in Mandy's direction. Caroline met his gaze impassively. Tony quickly turned away. Did he imagine a smile playing across Mandy's face? Miss Sandoval sat at her desk, face buried in the text.

Tony wrote something in his notebook, tore the page out, folded it, and neatly wrote "Mandy" on it in blue ink. He held the note out to Caroline. She raised one eyebrow, looking as if Tony had offered her something he had extricated from a sewer. Tony nodded towards Mandy. Caroline's eyes widened like saucers. Tony pointed to the note and then to Mandy. He again proffered it to Caroline, who took it and handed it to Miss Sandoval, now suddenly standing directly in front of Tony's desk.

Miss Sandoval opened the folded paper as Tony sank in his desk.

"I have admired you for the longest time. You are very beautiful and you have a cute..."

Miss Sandoval shook her head in disapproval.

"Oh, dear. Well, that's very flattering, Tony, however inappropriate."
The class erupted in laughter.

"Not quite up to the standards of "Endymion," but I'm sure your
fellows students will be happy to offer you some constructive criticism
after class. Now people, back to Mr. John Keats if you please!"

Tony buried his face in his hands.

That evening, the battered red 1998 Taurus that Silvan had produced
rolled across the International Bridge as the sun hung low and red just
over the horizon.

"Is there anything besides Loverboy to listen to? We're trying to
project cool here," complained Carson.

"It's cool, cuz," said Martin, always the first to deflect criticism
from his older cousin. "You okay back there, Tony?"

Tony had been scrunched down in the back seat since they passed
through the checkpoint, anxious not to attract attention to himself. He
stretched out a bit, looking around at the lines of cars and throngs of
vendors.

"Friday night in Nuevo Laredo!" Carson crowed. Silvan kept silent
as usual, barely acknowledging Tony. Silvan's standoffishness didn't
bother Tony terribly so long as he was not left alone with him.

"Hey, this is the place," said Martin, pointing at a mission style
building with white painted brick walls and a wrought iron gate in
front. "My aunt Edna's restaurant."

They entered to the strains of a jukebox playing loud *cumbia* music,
located a table near a cracked window and ordered. Later, after the
waitress cleared away their plates, Martin and Silvan excused themselves. Tony watched as they followed an older bearded man behind a
long polished counter at the back of the restaurant.

"Sweet food, huh?" beamed Carson.

"Is that one of Martin's Mexican cousins?" Tony asked.

"No doubt," replied Carson nonchalantly, without turning his
head to look. "Say, that chick over there is totally checking you out."

Tony sneaked a peak in the direction Carson was indicating. A
pair of Texas A & I coeds lavishly decked out for an evening on the

7

town sat at a nearby table, giggling and taking no apparent notice of either Carson or Tony.

"Come on, Carson! Those are college girls."

"Yes, but I happen to know that the gentleman prefers older women."

"I have no idea what you're on about right now, Carson."

"For example, Mrs. Livingston. People have noticed you staying late after class. Tongues are starting to wag." Carson smiled smugly.

"Man, don't even..." Tony sighed, exasperated at his friend's endless attempts to get a rise out of him.

"Got your mind set on someone else then? Caroline Montano, right?"

"Wrong."

"Come on, she has to be in the running. Where does Caroline Montano rank on the Tony Marco list?"

"I don't have a list! And if I did, Caroline wouldn't be on it."

"No?"

"If I had a list there would be a girl in Algebra that I haven't actually introduced myself to yet, a co-worker from a summer job two years ago..."

"Yeah?"

"...an internet friend from Japan. And Selena Gomez. Hey, I could meet her someday."

"And Mandy, who hasn't spoken to you since first grade?"

"It so happens I was talking to Mandy today. I think she's interested."

This was close enough to pure fabrication that Tony immediately regretted the boast, but Carson's eyes lit up with interest at the possibility of a germ of truth in Tony's words.

"Oh yeah? Slick. Got a date lined up?"

"Nah. Actually we just chatted for a while. But I think she might want me to ask her out."

"Possibly, possibly," Carson said, measuring his words and furrowing his brow as if concentrating on a problem of global importance. "But she could just want you as a friend. Do you want to be part of Mandy's he-harem of harmless boys?"

"Well, I figure I can get close to her by being her friend, and then..."

"No! That's the oldest mistake a brother can make. You can be the guy who brings her flowers every time her jerk boyfriend dumps her, be the guy who tells her jokes and makes her laugh, but at the end of the day you're just going to hear *thank you for being such a good friend*, and get a pat on the head for your troubles."

"So what do you do? Treat her like a jerk?"

"It's completely irrelevant how you treat her. Women know from the very start if they want you as a friend or more. You have to be able to read them."

Tony studied Carson, marveling at and perversely admiring his sheer ability to utter such pronouncements without a hint of self-consciousness.

"So, what are you reading from Mandy?"

"I never learned to read girls. I guess I'm girl-illiterate."

"Well, that's a lesson for another day, my man. Time to make the scene at that club. Lovely ladies are breathlessly waiting for you to request a dance. Let's not disappoint them."

"What about Martin and Silvan?"

"They can catch up. Anyway, if we get split up, we know where the car is. They're not going to abandon us."

Tony shrugged. "I know. Okay."

In the street outside the cool evening air carried a hint of adventure and subversive excitement. A lone guitarist paced down the sidewalk, stridently belting out "La Bamba" in a full-throated baritone while interpolating lyrics from a Katy Perry hit.

"It's this way," said Carson, gesturing.

"Hold on," said Tony, suddenly intrigued by one of the street vendor tents. Tony examined the odd array of old vinyl records, vintage lobby cards, toys, homemade pottery, woodcarvings, and novelty items. Carson reluctantly followed.

"Look at these," said Tony, eyeing a table lined with rows of exotically crafted brass charms and pendants. "This looks like something from medieval Scandinavia."

"Hey! Novelty celebrity driver's licenses! Shaq, Tom Cruise, Elvis! You must buy me one, son."

"Don't you have money?"

"I sprung for the fajitas."

"Oh, okay," replied Tony resignedly, as Carson jammed a stack of plastic cards into his hands.

Tony turned back to the vendor's table. An oval metallic pendant with a stylized wolf's head facing a dragon or monstrous serpent's head across a mountainous landscape caught his eye.

"That's a pretty one, eh?" said the vendor in stilted English. He was a white haired clean-shaven man, garbed in a faded military uniform of uncertain origin.

"I'm heading, bro," interrupted Carson.

"Okay, I'll catch up," Tony called back over his shoulder. He set the pendant down.

"Evil magician. Brought suffering for many," continued the vendor in a sorrowful tone, as if he was recounting something he had lived through.

"Hmm."

"One dollar," said the vendor.

Tony did a double take at the man, wondering if he had heard right.

The vendor smiled and nodded. "Just for you, young man."

Tony paid the man and without a further word pocketed the pendant and hurried off after Carson. He heard the vendor singing almost tunelessly to himself, *"And did she wear wildflowers in her hair...?"*

It was nearing 1:30 when Tony and Carson found their way back to the Taurus. Tony had practically dragged Carson out of the club, with increasingly alarmed pleas about how freaked out his mom was going to be.

"Son, you owe me big time. That girl was totally into me," boasted Carson as they made their way down the now mostly deserted street.

"You mean the one in the black and white dress and bob hairdo? She was dancing with everyone!"

"Just trying to make me jealous, son. You must understand the female mind. Hey, there's Martin."

"Where you been, buddies?" asked Martin, noticeably slurring his words as he leaned on the hood of the Taurus.

"No, no, no," said Tony, disbelievingly. "Were you guys drinking? Where is Silvan, anyway?"

Martin nodded at the car. Silvan was draped like a deflated balloon in the back seat, snoring.

"It's cool, man," said Carson. "They just wave you through the checkpoints. You're the man now, dog. To coin a phrase."

He grabbed the keys from Martin, who was just staring at the ground now, and dangled them in Tony's face.

"I'm not doing it."

"Come on, son. Time to snatch win from the jaws of fail."

"Great advice, Yoda."

"You drive, or my mom picks us up and drives us home," Carson stated flatly, holding up his cell phone with his other hand.

Tony had no answer to that. Carson's mother would certainly call his parents. In that event, Tony couldn't even begin to imagine what kind of fury would be unleashed upon him. It was bad enough he had skipped out on Arthur's party without explanation.

"Alright!" replied Tony, testily. He snatched the keys from Carson's hand. They piled into the car and Tony got behind the wheel. The music of Loverboy blared from the speakers as soon as the ignition turned over.

"What is the deal with this music!"

"The tape is stuck is the player," explained Martin, groggily.

"Just turn it off," said Carson, irritated. "Everyone be cool. They won't say anything if we just stay cool."

Tony drove the car up to a stop sign.

"Where do we go from here?"

"Just go straight."

"We'd be going the wrong way down a one-way street, Carson."

"This is Nuevo Laredo on a weekend! Who's going to care?"

"I'm going to try going right here."

Tony guided the Taurus through several more turns and found himself back at the same stop sign.

"Ugh, how do we get out of here? It's like that *Twilight Zone* episode where the train keeps returning to the same town."

"Left, left again, then right," directed Martin from the backseat. He unsuccessfully attempted to suppress a belch.

They finally reached the Mexican checkpoint. The officer on duty took one look at them, waved his hand and nodded.

"See?" said Carson. "Home free. Just don't flake out on us, son."

The dark waters of the Rio Grande lapped below as Tony guided them ever closer to the safety of the U.S. shore. A vague effluvial scent wafted in through the rolled-down windows of the Taurus. They passed through the U.S. checkpoint without incident. As he drove, Tony plotted how he could return without causing a commotion. Surely some party stragglers would still be littered about the yard by the time he got back, drunkenly belting out old *ranchero* songs. He could just wander around from the back and pretend that he had been there the whole time. Or if that didn't fly, he would just maintain that he was playing X-Box at Carson's.

"Watch your speed," cautioned Carson as they passed through Agua Dulce. They continued down Highway 44 through Robstown and finally past the Corpus Christi International Airport at the outskirts of the city. Orange fires from refineries blazed in the distance, ominous in the dark of the early morning. A 24-hour convenience provided a much needed bathroom break.

They agreed that Tony would drop the older boys off at Martin's house along with the car. From there, Carson and Tony would hike the remaining few blocks to their respective houses. Tony had never felt a stronger desire to be home and in his bed. The clock on the dashboard ticked inexorably past 2:30.

"Take this exit."

"I know the way," snapped Tony, annoyed at how Carson inevitably tried to take charge in every situation.

"Whoah, that light was nearly red, son."

Tony said nothing. Three more traffic lights would bring them to Orange Drive, the street they all lived on. Tony drove through the second light just as it switched from yellow to red.

"You'll never make the next one. That one always gets you."

Tony wasn't about to be stopped now. He accelerated and zipped through the intersection before the light had even turned yellow.

"You're the man, Tony!" crowed Carson.

"Woo!" called out Martin from the back, now getting into the spirit of it.

Tony laughed aloud despite himself.

The shrill sound of a siren nearly made Tony jump out of his seat. A sickening feeling overwhelmed him as he saw revolving red lights activate on the patrol car that had been laying in ambush in darkness by the side of the road. It pulled onto the road and closed on them rapidly.

"Oh, bummer," groaned Carson.

A helmeted police officer walked up to the driver's side window after Tony had pulled over.

"Evening," he said.

"Good evening, officer."

"Driver's license, please."

Everything seemed to turn dark in front of Tony's eyes. His spine fused and he found that he could not turn his head. Without thinking, he put his hand in his shirt pocket, as if a driver's license might somehow magically appear there. He felt something, had a flash of memory, and pulled it out.

The policeman studied the card and did a double take at Tony.

"Oh I'm sorry," he said in an apologetic tone. "I didn't realize it was you, Mr. Tom Cruise."

T wo weeks later, Tony made his way along the North Padre Island beach, weaving through children darting in and out of the surf, college students tossing Frisbees and footballs, and folding beach chairs occupied by pastel-clad retirees solemnly staring at the waves rolling in from the Gulf of Mexico. Tony's mother had reluctantly admonished him not to wander too far, but she had her hands full looking after two of her sister Sylvie's daughters. Tony's father had begged off the beach trip, staying behind to do a necessary inventory audit at the hardware store. Arthur had already rejoined his regiment in Okinawa. The outing had been planned for weeks, before Tony's Mexican adventure. Given the circumstances, Tony was not being trusted to stay home alone, so he had reluctantly tagged along, piling into his mother's old minivan with his young cousins.

Tony's parents had not reacted as severely as he had feared. Elena had quite a few choice words for him. Rudy, quiet as usual, had fixed him with a disappointed stare, which was somehow worse. Hearing that he was grounded for a month almost seemed a relief after the horrors Tony had envisioned lay in store for him, reform school chief among them. Fortunately, Elena had convinced the officer to let Tony off with a warning.

A flock of pelicans sailed overhead in formation, stately and unhurried, seeming to stand still in the air momentarily before banking towards the ocean. Tony watched as they retreated into the distance. A vaguely menacing bank of dark clouds had appeared over the horizon.

"Are you on the tour?"

"Huh?" asked Tony, startled. A young man with sandy blond hair dressed in a Tampa Bay Buccaneers football jersey and shorts stood before him. Something about him made Tony immediately desire his friendship.

"Yeah," said Tony finally, almost involuntarily.

"I thought so. I have one just like that," he said, gesturing at the wolf-and-dragon pendant that Tony was now wearing around his neck.

Tony's new acquaintance stared at him for a second and then grinned.

You were on the other shuttle, right?"

"Yeah, I was."

Having lied from the outset, Tony felt it would be awkward to retract his statement now.

"I'm Alexandre. With an "re" at the end," he added, giving Tony the sense that this was something he did reflexively every time he introduced himself.

"Tony."

"Cool. How are you liking it?"

Tony was momentarily puzzled by the question. Alexandre sensed Tony's confusion and made a circular motion with his head while raising his eyebrows, as if scanning the surroundings.

"Oh!" said Tony. "Yeah. It's alright you know. Pretty much the same thing every time. Jocks throwing footballs around, boogie boards, little kids digging with toy shovels throwing sand everywhere."

"Some pretty cute girls, huh?"

"Sure."

Alexandre laughed.

"Hey, we have a few minutes to grab a Coke before we have to go."

Alexandre gestured towards the refreshment stand by the parking lot and trotted in that direction. Tony followed. Once they had drinks, they sat at a small round wooden table shaded by an oversized blue umbrella.

"So this is BTDT for you, huh?" asked Alexandre. "It's my first time. My GF was here last year."

"Yeah?"

"We usually go to Vic England. You been?"

Tony had no idea what Alexandre was talking about, so he solemnly shook his head.

"Oh, I thought you might have," said Alexandre, sounding a bit disappointed. "I could have sworn I saw you there once. One of these days, when I've finished my Venetian lessons, we're going to try Ren-Eur. My mom's a total Ren junkie."

Something buzzed, and Alexandre reached into a pocket, drawing out what appeared to be a wafer-thin cell phone, which he studied intently for a moment.

"Our presence is being requested," he announced.

Alexandre leapt up and headed for the parking lot.

At this point, Tony knew that he should just admit that he was not part of whatever tour group Alexandre was a part of. But, aside from having to make that embarrassing confession, returning to his family, home, and grounding suddenly seemed like the last thing in the world he wanted to do. He trotted up behind Alexandre, who had queued up behind an older couple and a thin brunette woman in front of a short shuttle bus with "New Atlantis" and a stylized starfish logo painted on its side. The driver, a silver haired, mustached man who sported a wristwatch with a red leather band, greeted everyone as they filed in. Alexandre boarded before Tony.

"Hello, Mr. Marinos."

"Mister Alexandre," the bus driver responded, and then looked at Tony, who had been trying to avoid his gaze.

"It's okay. Tony's from the other shuttle," Alexandre explained.

Mr. Marinos studied Tony, and something flickered in his eyes. Recognition?

"Mister Tony! Climb aboard!"

Tony inwardly sighed as he took a seat next to Alexandre and watched other tourists file in. After an assortment of twenty-odd people, seemingly of all nationalities, had been seated, the shuttle bus departed the parking lot, drove down the beach access road, and onto the main highway.

Tony had almost worked up the courage to admit to the driver that he didn't belong in any tour group when he spied a young boy take a device out of a shirt pocket, press a button, and begin waving it in the air in front of him. A green globe, an inch and a half in diameter, appeared in the air. The boy made a motion as if he were swinging a racket, and the globe of light sped away and rebounded, like a ball attached by a rubber band to a wooden paddle.

"What?" asked Tony aloud.

"Ha!" said Alexandre. "I used to have one of those when I was a kid."

The thin brunette, who had taken the seat in front of Tony and Alexandre, was deep in conversation, apparently with her husband or boyfriend, but was not holding a phone. Tony peaked over the back of the seat and saw a sleek laptop device that was projecting a three-dimensional holographic image of the head and upper torso of the man she was bickering with. What had he stumbled onto? Tony felt panic at first. He snuck another quick peak around. Everyone appeared perfectly normal. Nothing seemed sinister. These were just tourists, after all.

"You okay, Tony?" asked Alexandre.

"Sure."

"BTW, you got your pass?"

"Um…"

"Are we spacing today?" asked Alexandre with a grin. "It's okay, use mine. My Dad works for the company."

He handed Tony a featureless silver-grey card.

"We're already at the stop."

Tony had hardly noticed when they had turned off South Padre Island Drive and onto a narrow tree-lined road. Now the shuttle was parking behind an old, derelict Gambler Mart. A larger bus that looked like the product of NASA technician design was parked next to a car wash stall.

"We're behind schedule! Ten minutes till jump! Restrooms inside if you need 'em." Mr. Marinos barked out, as the passengers de-boarded.

Tony watched as some of the passengers stepped into a secreted back door to the convenience store. Inside, past the boarded windows and sandblasted brick walls appeared a clean and well-ordered interior, stocked with beverages and snacks of all kinds in small silvery packets. Tony, overcome by curiosity, followed the other tourists in.

Something that appeared to be an animated map was projected on one wall, but Tony could not decipher its meaning. A revolving rack in one corner displayed an assortment of postcards. Tony picked one out that featured a typical tableau of golden sand dunes and seagulls hovering overhead. A sound of faint seabird cries and crashing surf emanated from the card. Had he also imagined the waves on the picture moving? Startled, Tony quickly put it back and heard a muted beeping sound as he did so.

Mr. Marinos took the opportunity to take a few noisy gulps from a red beverage he retrieved from the counter. He put his hand on Tony's shoulder.

"We need to get going, people. We have a tight schedule to run."

Tony had seen enough.

"Uh, Mr. Marinos, I think I need to wait for the other shuttle. My sister's on it."

"Other shuttle?" Mr. Marinos looked up at the schedule on the wall. "That won't be for another hour and a half."

"I can wait."

Mr. Marinos thought for a minute, brow furrowed in contemplation.

"Tell you what? Why don't I drive you back, and you can find your sister and catch the next shuttle?"

Tony looked doubtful. He spotted Alexandre stepping out of the restroom, heading his way.

"I don't want to impose…"

"It'll be fine," Mr. Marinos assured him. "This is my last run for the day. I'm just going back to the hotel after this. Anyways, I don't want to get you trouble for losing your sister."

"What's up?" asked Alexandre.

"Mister Tony here needs to pick up his sister. I'm driving him back to the shore."

"Oh. Alright, I'll catch you at the station later, buddy. My dad works there so I'm there most the time."

"Yeah. For sure."

He clasped Alexandre's outstretched hand.

"Boarding for Jump 344. Jump 344," blared a voice from outside.

The other tourists were already boarding the larger, rocket-like bus. Just as Alexandre turned away, Tony remembered the silver card he had given him. Tony opened his mouth, then closed it. Alexandre boarded the bus without a backwards glance.

The bus crawled into the car wash stall as Tony and Mr. Marinos watched from the door of the Gambler Mart. A low rumble was heard that grew to a throbbing roar. The ground shook. The vibrations seemed to reach inside Tony and shake his heart in his chest. Abruptly, there was something like a violent soundless implosion, soundless because it seemed that sound, light, air, and even color from the surrounding landscape had been sucked into the vacuum where the rocket bus had been.

"Uhhhh" said Tony, feeling queasy.

"Yeah, never get used to it," said Mr. Marinos sympathetically.

"Come on. Let's get back to the shore."

3

Little was said on the drive back. Tony sat in a near daze, wondering if he had somehow been made the butt of an elaborate prank. Mr. Marinos dropped him off with a kind word and drove off. He retraced his footsteps from the parking lot to the food and drink stand, back to where his mother and his cousins had entrenched themselves in the sand. Elena, surprisingly, hardly seemed to notice his tardy arrival. She fussed at the girls to retrieve their blankets and sand buckets. Tony estimated by the sun that only about thirty minutes in total had elapsed since he had first encountered Alexandre. Had the whole experience taken so little time?

That night, Tony turned in his bed and slept fitfully, lapsing into odd and disturbing dreams. At 3:30 in the morning he awoke and could not return to sleep for a full hour. As consciousness finally slipped away, he found himself hiking down a crooked footpath through a lightly wooded hilly area, seeming unlike anything in south Texas. Abruptly, the path led to a rocky cliff. Thin, bristling waterfalls on either side of him roared down seemingly thousands of feet down into a sea, the depth and expanse of which was shrouded in mist. On the promontory was built a foot-high quadrangle of stones, the ruins of a larger structure perhaps, from which ornate steps led to the edge of the cliff. Strange seabirds cried out songs of loss and loneliness as they winged overhead. A voice he couldn't recognize called his name and he awoke.

Two weeks later, after his grounding sentence had ended, Tony stepped off a city bus and made his way to the old Rio Theater downtown.

"Is Caroline Montano here?" he asked the girl in the box office booth.

The girl glanced back over her shoulder.

"Here she comes now."

A second later the door to the side of the booth opened and Caroline stepped out, leading an elderly man out by the arm.

"See you tomorrow, Mr. Preston."

"Good evening to you, Caroline," the man answered as he shuffled off to the bus stop, his cane clacking on the sidewalk.

Caroline didn't look surprised at all to see Tony.

"That man! He falls asleep every time he comes in here. One time I was working the late shift and we came that close to locking up when we realized he was still in there, snoozing away."

Tony said nothing at first, caught off guard.

"Hi Caroline. Nice uniform. I like the buttons."

"Huh?"

"Nothing."

"So what's new, Tony Marco? We haven't really talked in ages. What's up with that, anyways?" she asked, a hint of disapproval in the tone of her voice.

"Oh, gee. I don't know. It's just like...you know..."

"Yeah," she replied just icily enough to make Tony feel like a complete heel.

She sensed his discomfort and reverted to a normal conversational tone.

"We haven't hung in ages. I've missed my old bud."

"I've missed you too."

"So what's up?"

Tony exhaled.

"Can we go somewhere and talk?"

Fifteen minutes later Tony sat facing Caroline in a sandwich shop booth.

"Do they have shakes here?" she asked.

"I don't think so."

"Oh, darn. I wanted a shake."

Tony studied her as she took a hearty bite out of a turkey sub, melted American dripping from its end. She still wore her maroon Rio Theater jacket over a black shirt. Her black hair was shaved on the sides and pulled back into a short ponytail. Tony related his story from the time he first encountered Alexandre to his return to the beach on Mr. Marinos' shuttle.

"So, what do you think? Am I crazy?" he finally asked.

Caroline took her turn at studying Tony.

"It just...disappeared? In front of your eyes?"

"Yeah! Well, no! It drove into the car wash, and then it disappeared. I'm sure it wasn't there anymore, after all those flashing lights."

"Well, that's different! What do you think? Aliens? Spies?"

"No. They were just tourists. I'm somewhat mostly partially sure."

"So what are we gonna do?"

"Well, I was thinking, we should go back to that spot. See if they come back. Follow them around. See what they're up to."

"Great! Let's do it, man. Rock 'n' roll. Do you remember where the Gambler Mart is?"

"I think so, but it might be weird being asked to be dropped off at an old abandoned store on a deserted road."

"So what's the game plan, Kemo Sabe?"

"I was thinking we could just stake out that food stand and see if we can spot 'em. Then play it by ear. Can you get us there?"

"Yeah. All I have to do is ask my mom, and she'll take both of us. I think she's guilt-ridden from all those parenting books she reads. She worries that she's not there enough for me."

"What does your mom do anyways? Isn't she some kind of attorney?"

"She has a job with the Texas Department of Human Services, but she spends all her time working for Third World charities."

"Cool, I guess. My mom works with Child Protective Services. So tomorrow?"

"I'll give you a ring and we'll swing by and pick you up. Get your swim trunks ready!"

"Will do."

The next day Tony and Caroline walked side by side along the surf, heading for the spot where Tony had first met Alexandre. Caroline ran into the surf and dashed back out, chased by a wave, laughing. She wore cut-off blue-jean shorts and a pink sleeveless top, while Tony wore black cargo shorts and an unbuttoned loose orange flannel shirt over a school tee. His straight brown hair blew over his forehead in the breeze.

"Do you still hang out with that Carson guy?"

"Yeah. Sometimes. He can be a bit of a jerk."

"He called me "Hannah Montano" the other day. What is he, like twelve?"

Tony said nothing.

"Remember all those times when both our families would come out here? And that time when you were feeding the seagulls and you freaked when they started flocking all around you?"

"I did not freak out."

"You were actually running away!"

"Well, there were a lot of them. And they looked mean."

"Who's afraid of seagulls, Tony?"

"Hey, *The Birds* scarred me for life when I was a kid."

"Mmm-hmm."

"But I've made great strides since then. Just last month I watched a Woody Woodpecker cartoon and didn't even cover my eyes once."

"Ha ha! Very good, Tony. You'll go far."

"Hey, remember that time when you and Elizabeth…"

Tony caught himself.

"Hey," he said, halting in his tracks. "Are you alright? I'm really sorry about what happened to Elizabeth."

"It's okay," said Caroline, turning away. "It's been three years, almost."

Tony regarded her silently, not knowing what to say. Memories of Caroline's older sister flooded back. She had always been kind to Tony, soft spoken and graceful. Shortly after Elizabeth's abrupt death, Caroline's parents had moved out of the neighborhood. Tony later heard that they split up not long afterwards. It seemed so strange and puzzling to Tony, barely entering adolescence at the time.

"Hey, that's the place, right?" asked Caroline, pointing at the food and drink stand.

"Yeah," said Tony. "Come on. I'll buy you a pop."

"Pop," replied Caroline in a mocking voice. "Nobody says "pop" but you, Tony."

Tony went up to the counter and stood in line, while Caroline took a seat under one of the oversized umbrellas.

Tony heard the man in front of him ordering a hot dog and a soft drink. His blood chilled as he recognized the voice. It was Mr. Marinos! Tony was starting to back away when Mr. Marinos turned around.

"Mister Tony! Hello!"

"Hello, Mr. Marinos," he replied sheepishly.

"So you decided to stay for another couple of weeks, then?"

"Uh, yeah."

"Hello, Mr. Marinos!" said Caroline, suddenly at Tony's side.

"Hello! You must be Tony's..."

"Sister, yes. Is the shuttle almost ready to go? I've had enough of this old beach to last me a lifetime, let me tell you."

Tony stared wide-eyed at Caroline. She flashed back a nonchalant smile and jabbed him in the ribs.

Mr. Marinos glanced at his red-banded watch.

"Twelve minutes. You caught me just in time."

"Awesome! Let's go," said Caroline.

Again, Tony felt a prisoner of mysterious forces determined to toy with his life. Mutely he followed Caroline who eagerly ran up to the shuttle bus and hopped up the steps as soon as Mr. Marinos pulled open the doors.

❧ 4 ❧

Before Tony knew it, the shuttle bus was pulling into the parking lot of the same Gambler Mart, and he and Caroline had filed out with the handful of other passengers. After they had been allowed a brief restroom and refreshment break, Mr. Marinos herded them into line in front of the sleek rocket-bus.

"This'll never work," Tony hissed at Caroline.

The passenger in front of them held out a card as she boarded. A green cone of light shone out from a panel by the door and played over the card.

"Pass accepted for Jump 588," the disembodied female voice said.

"We've got to stop, now!" insisted Tony.

Caroline turned and looked at him, an annoyed glare in her eyes.

"Do you have the pass?"

Tony pulled it out of his shirt pocket. He had kept it close in the two weeks since Alexandre had given it to him for no rational reason he could express, save for possibly reassuring himself that he had not imagined the whole incident.

Before he could react, Caroline snatched it out of his hands and stepped up to the doorway of the rocket-bus. The cone of light shot out.

"Pass accepted for Jump 588."

"Caroline!" yelled Tony as she stepped forward. The green cone of light flashed again as he took a running step after Caroline. He felt a tingling sensation as it seemed to simultaneously scan him inside and out. Tony felt numbed and somewhat violated.

"Passenger L Anthony Marco recognized. Step forward, please."

27

Caroline seized Tony by the hand and hauled him forward through the doors of the bus. Still dragging Tony along, she led them to a pair of unoccupied seats.

"Please fasten your restraints and deactivate all electronic devices. The probability of a water landing is statistically nil, but in the extremely unlikely event this occurs, an inflatable seaworthy raft with a ten day supply of nutrients, universal positioning system, homing beacon, vid-phone, fishing implements, water desalinization system, and hybrid solar/electric battery engine is in the pouch in front of you. Jump to TS Khronos-Solarin in 2 minutes, 33 seconds."

Tony leaned over and whispered in Caroline's ear.

"There's no driver," he said.

"Yeah. Wild."

The bus had started moving of its own accord into the car wash stall.

"Are you kids alright?" asked an elderly lady sitting across from Tony and Caroline. She spoke in what Tony recognized as an Indian accent.

"This really helps for time sickness," she said, proffering a plastic bottle filled blue-green liquid.

Tony and Caroline looked at each other.

"No thanks!" they said in unison.

"Did she say time sickness?" whispered Tony.

"Jump in 5…..4….3….2……"

What followed next was something that Tony had trouble describing, even years later. There was a jarring sensation as of being abruptly cut off from something vital -- light, air supply, solid ground -- yet none of these things specifically. It seemed as if the world had somehow disappeared under his feet and in its place a great nothingness, something intangible but irresistible, was pulling him backwards into a great maelstrom below. He sensed that he was losing consciousness, even losing *existence*. Images began to flash in front of him. He found himself standing on a high cliff. Thin waterfalls on either side of him cascaded down the cliff into the sea. Did he know this place? A face appeared: an angry young man, not much older than Tony, wearing a silvery circlet. He yelled and gestured at him, but Tony couldn't hear the words, as he seemed to be receding and disappearing into a blur even as he spoke. Then Caroline appeared, dressed in an elegant white dress. She seemed...older? A worried expression crossed her features. He tried to call her, but as in a nightmare, the cry strangled in his throat.

"Caro...!"

Another jolting sensation.

"Jump completed successfully. Now docking with TS Khronos-Solarin, Gate 15B."

"...line," finished Tony, becoming aware of his surroundings and Caroline sitting next to him. Caroline's eyes were open but she seemed unaware of his presence. He patted her shoulder.

"Caroline! Snap out of it!"

She jerked into awareness. For the first time Tony saw something like concern in her eyes, but then a look of determination quickly took hold.

"I'm alright," she said.

The other passengers were already stirring, standing and stretching, some walking down the aisle towards the bus door.

"Let's go."

"Welcome to Time Station Khronos-Solarin," recited the disembodied female voice. "Station time is 13:44, October 6, 2088. Enjoy your stay at the station. Don't forget to visit the gift shop. If you enjoy authentic Asian cuisine from all eras, stop at the Huang-Karamov Diner. Need to whet your whistle? The Alexandrian has a seat reserved just for you."

Tony had some difficulty in getting up, as his legs seemed to temporarily refuse to support his weight, but soon found himself stumbling after Caroline out of the bus door and into a narrow corridor illuminated by a faint bluish light. The corridor opened into a wide, busy lobby, bustling with activity. People hurried back and forth down what seemed to be the main passageway in the station, some sat in rows of chairs, others stood in line in front of desks manned by personnel sporting identical navy-blue and white uniforms. A wall on the far side of the main passageway was entirely covered in a swarm of images; talking heads, schedules, news reports, and advertisements.

"Take care, dears," said the Indian lady, continuing on her way.

Caroline and Tony timidly stepped forward, drawn to the main passageway. The station appeared to be in the form of a large wheel or semi-circle, with the main passageway curving around a central hub. Small oval windows lined the length of the outer wall. It was dark outside.

A tween Asian girl approached, leading a terrier on a glowing leash. Abruptly she stopped, spoke a command, and the terrier dissolved in a haze of static and the leash shrunk into a tiny device in her palm. A man in an oddly dated looking suit and fedora stalked past, apparently carrying on a conversation with someone although he appeared to be alone. Several people sat in a bank of booths along the inner wall/ hub, wearing headgear that covered their eyes and ears. Letters reading "Cine-Sun" flashed above the booths. A group of formally dressed men and women glided past, apparently having skate wheels on the bottom on their otherwise normal looking business shoes.

"Did you see that?" asked Caroline excitedly, gesturing at a girl who skipped across their path. "She has hair like my cat! Like a …what do you call them? Orange tabby!"

Tony glanced at the girl, now standing in front of a man and woman dressed in black robes.

"I don't think that's a dye-job," said Caroline.

"I don't think so either," said Tony. "That looks like real fur."

They noticed a group of people gathered at one of the outer windows, staring out into the darkness. Tony and Caroline found an opening along the window and peered out.

"What?" asked Tony incredulously.

"Where are we?" asked Caroline.

"I think we're in space."

"Yeah. But what is *that*?"

Tony's eyes searched the darkness again. Then he saw it, or rather, *sensed* it. A nothingness, yet somehow tangible and foreboding, something that was unmistakably there.

"Can you feel that?" asked Caroline.

"Yeah. Like what we felt on the bus."

"I'm getting really freaked out right now, Tony."

Tony put his arm around Caroline, almost surprising himself with the tender gesture.

"It's alright. We're okay. We'll just look around for a while and go back the way we came."

"This really is the future, isn't it?"
"Yeah. I think so."

Caroline and Tony continued down the main passageway. They spotted The Alexandrian and what was either a museum or a clothing store. Startlingly lifelike animated mannequins modeled costumes ranging from Roman togas to 19th Century Plains Native American garb, to exotic uniforms from unfamiliar places and eras. Tony longed to see a friendly face, but Alexandre was nowhere in sight, and Mr. Marinos had never boarded the bus.

⤛ 5 ⤜

Proceeding cautiously, Tony and Caroline passed several more restaurants, stores and displays, and additional boarding and disembarking Gates.

"Whoah," said Tony.

A man whose eyes and ears were covered entirely by black plastic headgear approached.

"Can he see us?" asked Caroline, as the man took some halting steps towards them. Abruptly, the man stopped, smiled, and walked around them. Tony shrugged.

"Hey, look over there!" said Caroline, gesturing towards an arcade where people faced off against human and virtual opponents in various games and contests. Two girls batted an erratically moving glowing ball between them with what looked like stringless badminton racquets. In another corner of the arcade, they saw a young boy wearing oversized silver boots sparring with a spectral armored figure that floated around him, shooting green rays that the boy deflected with a fork-tipped staff he held. The boy suddenly leapt nearly six feet straight up, thrusting his staff through his virtual opponent, which vanished with a flash. Tony and Caroline observed with interest for several minutes, and then moved on. Eventually, they found themselves approaching the Gate they disembarked from, having made a complete circuit around the Station. Caroline slowed.

"I need to take a break, Tony," she said.

"Yeah," said Tony sympathetically. "I know what you mean." They were both physically and emotionally drained. Caroline leaned against a wall that was displaying a five-foot high image of a young woman's face.

33

"Need a break? Stop at Spiro's for a delicious latte," said the face, startling both Tony and Caroline.

Caroline spun around.

"Yes. I want something to drink," she said cautiously.

"Bring your family to Spiro's for a refreshing drink and a wide range of menu items for all tastes," the face continued impassively.

"It's just a program," said Tony. "Look, there's Spiro's over there."

They crossed the main passageway and found a small round table with stools on either side. A woman with green hair styled in bangs bustled up to them.

"Are you ready to order?"

"I'll have an orange soda," said Caroline. Tony noticed that Caroline was reading menu items that were appearing directly on the table surface.

"And you?"

"Uh, just water."

"Coming right up, sweetie."

"How are we going to pay?" hissed Tony as the waitress hurried away.

"I figured it out when we were in the Gambler Mart! You didn't see anyone pay for anything, did you?"

Tony shook his head.

"No, they just picked up what they wanted," Caroline continued, "and there was a beep. It's the passes! Somehow they immediately record the purchase."

She pulled the pass out of her shorts' pocket.

"Watch and learn."

The green-haired waitress returned with their drinks, placed them on the table, and walked off without a word. Tony heard a faint but distinct beep. Caroline grinned in satisfaction.

"So what are we going to do now? Won't it look weird if we just ask to go right back?" asked Tony. "And they'll also notice if we just hang around here for too long."

"What will they do if they bust us?" mused Caroline. "Will they keep us here forever? Will they wipe our memories?"

"Maybe we should just come clean. Turn ourselves in to the authorities -- whoever they are. I mean, what can they do? These people aren't savages. Mr. Marinos was really nice."

"Bad idea," said an unfamiliar voice.

They turned and saw a man standing by their table. He had shoulder-length dark hair, a thin moustache, and wore brown trousers, well-worn boots, and a loose-fitting black shirt with ornate silver buttons.

Tony and Caroline glanced at each other in panic.

"Relax, kids," said the man, pulling a chair from a nearby table in a fluid motion and sitting facing them. "I'm a friend."

Tony and Caroline said nothing.

"I noticed you from the moment you disembarked," the man continued. "I could tell you were lost. I've been there before."

He held out his hand to Tony.

"I'm Stephen. Stephen Gaudet," he said gently.

Tony cautiously grasped his hand. Caroline nodded in his direction but did not offer her hand.

"And you are...?"

"He's Tony and I'm Caroline," she said flatly, in a tone that made it clear that she was not interested in volunteering any more information than necessary.

"Very well. Tony. Caroline," continued Mr. Gaudet. "I won't even ask how you found yourselves here. I'm not gonna pry into your lives. I did the same thing, years ago. I'm from your time, more or less. That's how I could tell you didn't belong here."

He paused and glanced at Tony's school tee-shirt.

"Corpus Christi, Texas," he read.

Tony flinched and closed his flannel shirt over his chest, as if the mysterious stranger might read more details of his life there.

"I'm a Cajun boy from Lake Charles, myself." A bit of an accent began to creep into his voice. "Born in '51. Sixteen years ago a sweet little lady I met in San Francisco took me for a ride I'll never forget and I wound up here. That was 1969. Yes, for me it's been sixteen years since 1969 – near as I can figure at least. Time travel confuses things. Believe me, it gets even more confusing."

He paused again and seemed to study Tony and Caroline.

"You, I'm guessing 2012. 2015?"

He raised his eyebrows. Tony had started to nod, almost involuntarily.

"Ah. I thought so. But I'm not prying. Not prying. You see, I still make runs to the 20th and early 21st century. Now let me tell you why turning yourself in is a bad idea."

6

Gaudet pushed his chair further in and lowered his voice to a conspiratorial whisper.

"Time travel is regulated, you see. Tightly regulated. The folks at Temporal Affairs don't want people messing around where they don't belong, unless there's someone to keep a close eye on them. They kept me for "observation" for months, until they were sure that I wouldn't go back to my time and expose their operations to the world."

"But they let you return."

"Eventually they did just that, after keeping me on a tight leash and indoctrinating me with their "moral time travel" propaganda. Ultimately I decided that this era had more to offer me, so I stayed. Once you reach a place where trivial things like decades -- or even centuries -- are no longer an obstacle to where you want to go, what you want to see, what you want to do in life, it's hard to go back. You might wrestle with the same dilemma yourselves one day, if you stay here long enough."

"I think I've seen enough," said Caroline pensively. "I just feel like I don't belong here. I shouldn't even be seeing these things."

"You, Tony?"

Tony shrugged diffidently.

"So, exactly how much have you figured out about this place by yourselves now, by the way?"

"It's Twenty Eighty…Eight," began Caroline.

"This is a Time Station where you can go back in time to different periods in earth's history," continued Tony. "And we're in space right now."

"And that?"

Gaudet nodded at the window where people peered into the forbidding darkness.

"It's a black hole. This station somehow harnesses its power to hurtle people back in time."

"Very good Tony, my man," said Gaudet. "I could tell you were a bright one. But that's a simplified explanation. Once energy enters the event horizon of a black hole, it's never coming back, at least not in any manner that can be controlled. This station has a giant collector that intercepts energy pulled in by the black hole, which is then used to power travel through time."

"What about the Time Bus, or whatever that was?" asked Caroline. "It didn't have a driver."

"Care to hazard a guess, Tony?" asked Gaudet.

"Well, I would think that time travel would mess up the instrumentation, navigation somehow. So it's controlled remotely. From this station?"

"Bingo!"

"Can you travel back in time and come back before you arrived?"

"Let me ask you this, Caroline: can you be in two places at the same time? Because if you arrived right before you left you'd be face to face with yourself, wouldn't you?"

"I guess you couldn't."

"See, think of this table as the whole of time. Right now, you're here." He gestured to where Caroline's orange soda sat. "But if you jump back to say, 365 B.C., you're here." He indicated a spot several inches to the right. "Just as if you'd suddenly appeared a few feet down the corridor here. You're here and then you're there. And then you pop back to where you were originally. But you can't be two places at the same time. It's not just a violation of the rules of time travel; it's a violation of all the rules of physics."

"But you can come back a second after you left," broke in Tony.

"Less than a second."

"What about the danger of changing history? I read that story where someone stepped on a butterfly and it changed everything. Isn't that something these people worry about?"

"Ah, interesting question, Caroline. Interesting question. And to answer it, it's better to not think of time as a line or string. You can't grab one end of the string and yank it and pull the rest of the string in a new direction. Time is not a line, but more like a plane you're on. The invention of the wheel is here and, look over there! It's the first manned voyage to Mars. Look back over there and William the Conqueror is leading a band of Norman cavalry against the Anglo-Saxon forces of King Harold II in England. All in one interconnected tapestry of events that we could never truly grasp in an eternity with our limited faculties, one moment flowing into the next. When you go back in time, you're jumping from one place to another like a flea could hop all over this table, but you're not stopping the flow. It doesn't work that way. Nothing gets rewound or replayed; everything is already in motion. Because you're part of the tapestry."

"So when you go back in time..." began Tony.

"Uh huh?"

"You're not rewinding the clock. Things aren't happening again. You're a part of the events. You..."

He hesitated.

"Go on," urged Gaudet, sounding amused.

"You were always part of the events, in the past. When you jump back, you become part of the chain of events. You were always part of it."

"Now is your mind blown?"

Tony and Caroline both nodded.

"Yeah."

"Uh-huh."

The waitress returned to their table to ask if they wanted anything else, but Gaudet waved her off.

"So why the need for regulation?" asked Tony. "You can basically do anything that you want to in the past, and it just becomes part of history?"

"Ah, that's where the "moral" component comes in. What if you go back in time and shoot someone? It's part of history. But is it right? Or someone could go back in time with their knowledge of the future and live like a monarch, taking advantage of poor, ignorant souls of some benighted era of the past. It happens. There are rogue time travelers who do just that."

"But how do they slip past?" asked Tony. "Do they just jump off the bus and don't get back on?"

"Not all time travel is controlled through this station. This is just a station for time tourists. Other stations are set up for scholars, for "time explorers" if you will, for research. I'm a bit of an explorer, myself. The organization I'm with scouts different time periods that might be suitable for tourism. Officially, that's the province of Temporal Affairs, but so far what we're doing isn't technically illegal. There are ways to slip through the nets, to avoid Temporal Affairs' oversight. Looks like you two did just that. And I'm thinking you need my help to get back, if you don't cotton to the idea of being stuck here for a long, long time."

Gaudet paused, seeming deep in thought.

"I can get you out. Below the radar, so to speak. I have my own shuttle, controlled from our own base. I dock here from time to time out of necessity, on company business, but I'm not controlled from here. Our base will transmit a time/flight plan to Temporal Affairs. The Temps will rubberstamp it 'cause our record is clear and they already have a presence in your time. You two come along as my passengers and no one here asks questions, 'cause we're an independent agency. It's not Khronos-Solarin Station business anymore. Paperwork, such as it is in this time, can be filed at my firm's base to clear you with the Temporals. I know people at the Firm who owe me favors and won't ask."

Caroline turned to Tony. Tony could sense her concern.

"Can we talk it over?" asked Tony.

"Talk it over as long as you like, kids," replied Gaudet. "Me, I'll be at Casey's. I like the drinks there better. A little more kick, you see."

With that Gaudet rose and exited without a backward glance. Tony and Caroline watched as he disappeared down the main corridor. When he was out of sight, Caroline turned back to Tony.

"Tony, I don't want to stay here. I mean, it was great seeing all this, but I - we - don't belong here. It's too much for me. I want to go back to my room. To my Mom. To my job."

"Yeah, I know what you mean. But do you trust this guy?"

"Mister Cajun hippie? No. Did you notice how he suddenly had an accent when he found out we're from Texas? And all this "not technically illegal" stuff and fixing paperwork...I just don't know, Tony."

"We could just try to board the next bus back to our time. It worked one way."

"Yeah, but at that end it was just Mr. Marinos, who assumed we were supposed to be on the bus back to the Station. Maybe the pass only works for one trip, for all we know. And won't we immediately draw attention to ourselves asking to go right back? Someone will notice."

"And if they discover the truth, the Temporal Affairs people might never let us return to our own time. If Mr. Gaudet never returned..."

Tony trailed off. He imagined his parents wondering where he had disappeared, agonizing perhaps for the remainder of their lives over his fate.

"I think we have to trust him. I don't think he's lying to us about being able to get us home."

"Do you have one of your feelings? I've always trusted your feelings."

Caroline searched for reassurance in Tony's eyes.

"Yeah. I've got one of those feelings."

"Okay. That's good enough for me."

They located Mr. Gaudet at Casey's, sitting with a drink in front of him, lost in reverie.

"Mr. Gaudet," said Tony tentatively, as if gently trying to rouse someone from slumber. "We've decided to accept your offer."

Gaudet turned, looking at them almost as if he were seeing them for the first time.

"Tony. Caroline. I will be honored to help you."

He held out his hand to Tony, who clasped it. Caroline shrunk away.

"Caroline, you have my word, as a Cajun gentlemen, that I will return you safely back to your home."

Caroline hesitated, and then finally accepted his proffered hand.

"Excellent. I've already called ahead to my people. They'll have us cleared by the time we get to my shuttle. So if you've had quite enough of the year 2088, I suggest we leave forthwith."

⇜ 7 ⇝

G audet led Caroline and Tony down a previously unnoticed side corridor. A panel swished open, revealing a sleek craft that looked like a cockpit with fins attached. They entered through a hatch in the rear.

Gaudet strapped himself into a swiveling chair at the fore of the craft, pressed an octagonal icon on a screen in front of him and spoke.

"Khronos-Solarin control, this is Shuttle 3BH. Requesting clearance for jump."

"3BH stand by. Confirming flight plan. Do you have passengers?"

"Yes, indeed. Please check LC-Veston flight plan transmission."

"Verifying...Roger. You're looking at an approximate fifteen minute queue prior to jump clearance. You may disengage from the lock and taxi to prepare for jump. Do not, repeat do not enter the jump zone until cleared."

"That is most satisfactory, Kronos-Solarin," replied Gaudet. "Strap in, kids. No artificial gravity once we're free of the Station."

Tony and Caroline found two padded seats positioned behind Gaudet's, each equipped with a harness system that automatically locked firmly but comfortably across the chest and waist.

"Here we go," said Gaudet, inhaling loudly.

Tony felt a mild jolt. There was a sense of movement followed by the somewhat disconcerting sensation of weightlessness.

"Whoah," said Caroline.

"Yeah, this feels weird," said Tony.

"Not that," said Caroline, "*That*."

43

She pointed to the window in the fore of the cockpit. The full length and breadth of the Khronos-Solarin Time Station loomed in front of them.

"It's bigger than anything I've ever seen," gasped Caroline.

Now fully visible as it floated in space, the station was revealed to be in the shape of an immense wheel, with a complex latticed metallic framework connecting the outer hoop to a small central hub. From the central hub projected a long axle with massive sieve-like structures at either end, each almost as wide as the outer hoop of the station itself. Light streamed out from seemingly thousands of windows. Projecting from the outer hoop were dozens of spires, all with a variety of reflective discs and antennas affixed. One imposing structure stood out among the others, looking for all the world like a control tower at an airport. The station rotated beneath them, a world in its own right, as the shuttle hovered over its surface.

"Thought you might enjoy that," commented Gaudet, chuckling.

"It looks kind of Art Deco," said Tony.

"Ah, those silly 2070's," sighed Gaudet.

"Mr. Gaudet," asked Tony, "What's the world like now? I mean in this time. If people can build something like this in space..."

"There have been some dramatic advances, no doubt," answered Gaudet, in a thoughtful tone. "Some of the sights would not suffer in comparison to the Seven Wonders of the Ancient World, not the least that time station floating before your eyes. There are underwater cities. A permanent base on Mars is in the works."

"Things must have really changed since our time."

"In some ways yes. Probably not in the ways you might expect though. In many ways, life is just the same."

"Are there still countries? Wars?"

"Old national borders don't fade quickly as you should know, but wars these days -- aside from some tense moments now and again – they're more like internet flame wars."

Tony was not satisfied with Gaudet's answer, but didn't press the subject.

"Do people go back to time of dinosaurs?" asked Caroline.

"Only the scientists. No tourists allowed in...dangerous times."

"Oh, that would be so cool, to see dinosaurs."

"How about you, Tony? You want to be face-to-face with a T-Rex sometime?"

"Ah, I don't know. That might be kind of scary."

"Don't need that much excitement in your life? Do you want to lead a comfortable life, or an interesting life?"

Tony chuckled in embarrassment.

"This is pretty interesting," he replied.

"I'll bet you've led an interesting life," said Caroline.

"That I have, Caroline. That I have. And I reckon I'll be content in that knowledge when I'm standing before my maker one day. You believe in the Afterlife, Tony?"

"Oh, I don't know. I guess, but I don't think it's like people say, where they replay all the bad things you've done in life. What do you believe, Mr. Gaudet?"

"Well, the fact is that I have converted to a new religion of these times, the Church of the Statisticians. Statisticians believe that when you die, you aren't judged. However, you get to review all the statistics of your life; the exact number of grains of rice you ate, how many people fell in love with you that you never knew about, how much money you lost, the percentage of grain cereal you ate that was actually rat droppings or insect larvae, the number of kilometers you've walked, how many hours of other people's time you wasted, and so on. See? I told you life has changed in ways you could not have expected."

"You're putting us on, Mr. Gaudet."

"That I am. Can't put nothing past you."

"Do people live longer now?" asked Caroline.

"Average life expectancy has increased somewhat with medical advances, as you might imagine, but not that dramatically."

"Do people travel to the future?"

"It's only possible to travel to the past."

"But *we* traveled to the future. And you did too."

"Good point, Tony my man. When someone, or something, gets displaced in time, it's like a rubber-band being stretched. People and things are tethered to their general time-frame. You caught a ride on a time bus that was being pulled back to its tether point."

"But if we're tethered to our time..." began Caroline.

"You would eventually return to your time spontaneously."

Caroline gasped.

"Except there is a temporal stasis field generated by the station that will keep you here as long as you are in range. Every time bus or shuttle generates its own stasis field that will keep the rebound effect in check until its passengers are ready to return. Time tourists can't stray too far from a designated area where the field is in effect. You don't want to get swooped. That's what they call it: getting "swooped" back to your time. Now, if you were to spend ten years in the "non-native" time frame, you would naturally be drawn to your tether point ten years after your left, give or take."

"What would happen to you if you got swooped?"

"Well, to be truthful only a few accounts exist. A young and strong person like you who is prepared for it physically and mentally could probably survive a swoop with few ill effects. But imagine what tumbling head over heel through a maelstrom of all time and all reality could do to a body. And mind."

"Does anyone visit this time from the future? I mean the future for 2088?" asked Caroline.

"It's only been known to happen once," answered Gaudet without elaborating.

"There was something weird we saw on the station," said Tony. "A man walking around with this dark headgear. I wasn't sure that he could actually see us, but somehow he sensed us."

"Hmm. He could have been blind. There are glasses and headsets that allow visually impaired people to navigate, kind of like radar. Most cases of blindness can be easily cured now, though. He might have just been ignoring everyone on purpose. The same technology can be used to block out people you don't want to see or hear, just as you would put someone on "ignore" on your computer at home."

"Shuttle 3BH," a voice from the control tower broke in, "Prepare to enter jump zone and transfer to remote guidance."

"Understood," replied Gaudet. He turned back to Tony and Caroline and said, "Here we go," while maneuvering the shuttle away from the station.

"3BH, this is LC-Veston Control. Prepare for jump in forty-five seconds…thirty seconds…fifteen seconds…ten…five, four, three, two, oooooonnnnnnnnneeeee…"

Again, a dreamlike jumble of images, then a feeling of falling into nothingness, and blacking out followed by the same disconcerting feeling as when one wakes up in an unfamiliar bed when traveling, compounded several hundred times over.

"We're here," announced Gaudet, as if from miles away.

"Where...are we?"

"A remote area. A blind. We couldn't just plop down in the middle of the city, after all, and we can't use Temporal Affairs' facilities. We've got a bit of a hike, I'm afraid."

Gaudet pulled a lever and the shuttle's hatch popped open. Sunlight spilled in, hurting Tony's eyes.

"Let's go," said Gaudet, stepping out.

Tony and Caroline followed Gaudet out of the hatch, blinking. The shuttle had landed in the middle of a clearing in a wooded area.

"Ooh, it's chilly," complained Caroline. How far do we have to walk?"

"A fair bit, Caroline. This way!"

He gestured to a gap in the ring of surrounding trees, where a rutted path was visible through the grass and brush.

"This doesn't look right," said Tony, examining their surroundings. "These trees..."

"What's that sound?" asked Caroline.

A rumbling sound in the distance became discernible as galloping hoofs. Through the gap in the ring of trees rode two men on horseback. They stopped mere feet in front of them, kicking up a storm of dust on the path.

"What's going on, Tony?" asked Caroline worriedly.

Tony looked up at the two riders. Both wore brown Brigandine armor with a stylized wolf's head design on the cuirass. Gaudet stepped to one side. Incredulously, Tony watched as one of the riders pulled a long thin sword out of his saddle and pointed it directly at his nose. There was no doubt that it was real, made of heavy polished steel.

"Gaudet!" the rider called out, "Are these the ones?"

"They be, indeed."

"You're in the sovereign domain of the Wolf King now, heathens."

"Welcome to the 11th Century," said Gaudet with a cruel laugh.

"But," said Tony, "That's *impossible!*"

⊰꙳ 8 ꙳⊱

The Fort of the Three Hills had been built by a man of high birth among his people, known as "The Ravenous" for his prodigious appetite. As a young man he had made his fortune in Galloway. On the night of his wedding, the Ravenous One had experienced a vivid dream in which he beheld a distant, verdant land where three hills stood side by side. Believing it an omen, he and his wife along with 319 loyal men and relatives set out, seeking the Vision Land. When three pointed peaks were spotted in a fair-seeming pastoral new land, the Ravenous One was convinced that he had been divinely guided. His people built the fort in the shadow of these peaks in the manner of their people, and set their wills to taming the surrounding countryside. They fished and hunted, grazed their cattle, and harvested the bounty of the land. At the onset of the first winter, the Ravenous One called for feasting and prayer to the Christian God.

In the second year, a secondary outpost was built near a narrow part of the small river where fishing was good. By this time, increasingly hostile forays and ambushes by the strange men of that country had upset the settlers' newfound contentment. In the first month of the second winter, the Ravenous One was slain during a raid by the strangers. Another small lookout post was built on a hill in the woods with an unobstructed view of the surrounding countryside.

The second winter proved to be harsh and the third nearly disastrous, with unforgiving snows and a deadly dearth of food. Most of their cattle died, and the rest had to be slaughtered to feed the people of the Fort. In a time of desperation, the wife of the Ravenous One, who at best paid lip-service to the Christian God, sought the advice of a Seeress skilled in the old wisdom of their folk. They gathered at the Stone of Song near the willow pond, and the Seeress there made her pronouncements. When asked if their descendents would still inhabit this land in years hence, the Seeress replied that it was so. However, that night, the wife of the Ravenous One had a dream in which she saw a devouring wolf with monsters in his train descending on the land.

The people, knowing nothing of this dream, were somewhat set at ease by the words of the Seeress, but their fortunes did not improve. Food remained scarce and the strangers proved to be intractable. The nephew of the Ravenous One, now risen to power and prominence, sowed discontent among the people and eventually convinced most of their folk to follow him back to the home country, against the wishes of the wife of the Ravenous one. The remaining few held out for some months but ultimately perished or fled. Returned to her home country, the wife of the Ravenous One soon allied herself with another man of influence, but he angered the king and fell from favor. The wife, now called the Ill-Starred, was shunned and no one would heed her entreaties to return to the land of the three hills. And so the Fort was abandoned for a time.

❧❀❀☙

Gaudet bound the bands of Tony and Caroline with coarse rope while the horsemen held them at sword-point.

"Let me go, you Cajun hippie freak!" Caroline protested and then unleashed a torrent of profanity that surprised even Tony. Gaudet just chuckled.

"Now, march," ordered one of the horsemen. Caroline and Tony were prodded onto the rutted path leading out of the clearing. Before long, the elm, maple and brush growth thinned and they found themselves in a bucolic landscape, where cows and sheep grazed on sloping green fields in the distance. A small river wound away to their left, widening until it lazily drained into marshlands. The path before them eventually narrowed into a thin, sandy land bridge. They continued onto a forested peninsula, headed towards three imposing rocky hills thrust up side by side. In the shadow of these triplet hills lay an austere rectangular wood and stone structure with extensive fortifications sprawled around it.

"Selwys Castle," proclaimed Gaudet, dramatically.

As they marched along, the trees gave way to muddy, smelly, trodden earth surrounding the castle. A sharp outcropping of granite, six feet tall at its highest point, erupted from the earth like the claw of some monstrous creature pointing at the three hills.

Tony was starting to tire as they trudged across a narrow wooden bridge straddling a deep dry ditch and through the outer gate into the castle complex. Inside the gate, men turned and stared inquisitively at the captives. The horsemen dismounted and escorted Tony and Caroline up a set of flat stone steps into the main building. The air grew chilly and torches mounted on the wall offered no warmth. Once past the foyer, they were led through a hallway and into a wide, low-ceilinged chamber. Within, a dark haired young man crowned with a thin silver circlet was perched on an ornate, cushioned throne. Behind him, a wide tapestry with the now-familiar wolf's head insignia hung. The floor was painted in a checkerboard design. To one side stood a frail but cruel looking young man with wispy blond hair. In the center of the chamber, a bearded elderly man sat playing an instrument Tony recognized as a lute, singing in a high, wavering voice. A pale woman with striking blue eyes dressed in a diaphanous off-white gown twirled in time to the music with an oddly disinterested expression on her face. Tony noticed other people lurking in the corners of the chamber as his eyes became accustomed to the torchlight. Gaudet and the horsemen guided Tony and Caroline to one side of the chamber. The attention of everyone in the room seemed focused on the song and dance.

Caroline turned to Tony.

"What's going to happen now?" she whispered.

"Just wait. Something is off about this. All of this."

"Do *not* speak until spoken to," hissed Gaudet.

Eventually the song ended. The lute player rose, genuflected to the young man on the throne and exited the chamber. The pale woman took a place next to the frail blond man.

"Were you pleased, Milord?" she asked in a bored voice.

"Nay, Milady Neon Sparrow," said the dark haired man. "The melody was repetitive and there were too many verses. Surely more talented minstrels can be procured to perform for the Court Royal?"

No one responded.

"Very well," the young man grumbled, "What's next on the agenda?"

"There's a juggler from the servants' camp," said the frail young man.

"A juggler, M'lord," said the woman referred to as Neon Sparrow.

"Another juggler? Is that the best we can do now, people? Send him away."

"Send the juggler back to the camp!" called out one of the horsemen.

"I believe we had some items of business on the agenda," said the frail young man.

"Okay, what's next?"

"The castle staff wanted a swimming pool," said Neon Sparrow.

"Oh yes. Well, I already said they could have a pool if they fill the ditch with water. Is it that difficult to get a decent moat? Where are we on that project?"

"Sir Penultimate Theorem was making some progress on diverting water from the river. Weren't you, Sir Penultimate Theorem?" She turned to the frail young man.

"As soon as we can spare some men from the harvest..." he began.

"As soon as men can be spared from harvesting crops, they will finish the project," finished Neon Sparrow.

"Very well. Finish the project and they have their pool."

"Am I to understand then, Milord, that an actual swimming pool will be constructed on the castle grounds?"

"Did I say that? I said they could swim in the moat."

"You did not."

"I most certainly did. Court Reporter! Replay my statements on the matter!"

"16 July, 1033, 7:23 P.M.; Wolf King: *They want a pool now? They can have a pool if they fill the* [expletive deleted] *moat with water.*"

Tony looked around the room but did not see anyone speaking. The disembodied voice continued.

"21 September, 1098, 6:12 P.M.; Wolf King: *Oh yes. Well, I already said they could have a pool if they fill the ditch with water.* 3 October, 1098, 9:45 A.M.; Wolf King: *Very well. Finish the project and they have their pool.*"

"ROFL," murmured Neon Sparrow.

"Well, never mind that," broke in the young man known as the Wolf King, "It's clear what I meant. Why is the swear guard engaged on the Court Reporter?"

"It's the default setting, Milord. Default *pud-duh, pud-duh* default."

"Did you say, *pud-duh*? I will not have *pud-duh* in my court! Next matter of business!"

"There was the matter of plum rations."

"Isn't this another old matter? I distinctly recall saying that if Vanaya increased production by fifty bushels, rations would be increased."

"Court reporter!" commanded Neon Sparrow, "Replay the Wolf King's statements on the matter!"

"31st April, 1098, 7:42 P.M.; Wolf King: *That's what Kinnemort reported. If they increase production by twenty-five bushels, I'll allow it.*"

Neon Sparrow grinned triumphantly.

"Oh very well."

"You are most gracious, Milord."

"Next?"

"I believe we have apprehended one of the escapees," responded Sir Penultimate Theorem.

"An escapee, Milord," echoed Neon Sparrow.

She gestured towards the entrance through which Tony and Caroline had previously entered, and two more armored men entered, holding a bedraggled man by each arm. They dragged him to the center of the chamber.

"Farlowe? How could you? I must say I am disappointed." The Wolf King stood and took a step forward towards the man.

"How do you plead, scum?" sneered Sir Penultimate Theorem.

"I will not plead," responded the captive. "Nor will I play the sick games of a pretend King anymore."

The Wolf King looked visibly stunned for a moment, then quickly composed himself. Tony wondered if he had imagined a hint of a smirk on the face of the young lady called Neon Sparrow.

"Well, I am truly sorry you feel that way, Farlowe. I thought we had an understanding. I mean, what else do you people want? Am I not the most generous of monarchs? Do I not give my subjects everything they need?"

"The Wolf King is magnanimous," recited Neon Sparrow flatly.

The captive man remained silent.

The Wolf King frowned.

"Well, to the Drake with you."

He grasped a short fork-tipped lance mounted near his throne. A blinding beam of light shot out from it, gradually engulfing the armored men and their captive as a great droning noise filled the chamber. Abruptly, there was simultaneous darkness and silence. When Tony's eyes adjusted, the bedraggled captive was gone. He heard Caroline gasp beside him.

"Hmm," murmured Tony,

The Wolf King turned his gaze to the corner of the chamber where Tony and Caroline stood. "Sir Gaudet! I believe you bring prizes for me?"

"That I do, my Lord. That I do."

One of the horsemen roughly pushed Tony and Caroline from behind. They took a couple of halting steps forward, warily eyeing the young man called the Wolf King.

"Well, what do we have here?"

"Tony and Caroline," said Gaudet. "More driftwood in the time-stream."

"Eh. Not very interesting looking. Don't think I can use them for anything but laborers around the castle grounds. Though the girl isn't hideous. Maybe I'll have her for my court."

"If you even touch her..." Tony began.

"You stinking piece of..." said Caroline.

Suddenly, there was a blinding flash and Tony felt as if his legs had lost their ability to support his weight. He fell to his knees alongside Caroline, who struggled and toppled with an anguished sound. When Tony opened his eyes, he saw the Wolf King pointing his lance at them.

"You will learn your place in the Kingdom of the Wolf," snarled Sir Penultimate Theorem.

Neon Sparrow looked on with sudden interest. She turned to the Wolf King.

"Milord, the girl is too plain for this station and obviously ill-favored. It would please me to see her laboring in the fields."

The Wolf King was silent for a moment.

"Very well. If it pleases you, it will please me."

He turned to Tony.

"And where does this one belong? Too bookish looking. Wouldn't give the dragon much sport. Too tall for Doren's people. Too dark for Vanaya's clan. And much too old at this point anyways."

"I know where you belong," said Tony. "Not here, that's for sure."

The Wolf King's eyebrows raised.

"Hush!" warned Gaudet.

"This Old Timer thinks he is clever," replied the Wolf King contemptuously. "If you are as smart as you fancy yourself, you will learn to accept your fate. There is no escape from the Temporal Proprietary of the Wolf."

He returned to his throne and sat.

"Take this trash out of here."

❧ 9 ❧

C aroline and Tony were escorted out of the Wolf King's courtroom by one of the horsemen, out through the same entrance
and down the steps, and back into the main enclosure of the
fort. They marched past several animal pens to a long wooden building positioned alongside one length of the outer fence. Two more
similar structures also lined the fence at even intervals.

"This is your new home," said the horseman with a cruel sneer.
"You will learn the routine here soon enough. Hey boy!"

He called out to a blond bespectacled boy of around twelve who
stood in an almost catatonic state facing the outer fence.

"These are new laborers. Make yourself useful and show them the
ropes."

The boy turned and stared at Tony and Caroline in wide-eyed
wonder.

"Inside, all of you," said the horseman. "The hour grows late." He
glared at them and then turned, abruptly seeming to lose all interest
in the young prisoners.

Tony and Caroline mutely returned the boy's stare.

"Well, come on then," said the boy. "There's no getting out. The
fences are charged, even if you could climb them. We'll have some
supper in a bit."

"Is there a restroom in there?" asked Caroline. "I kinda need to..."

"Yeah, me too," added Tony.

"There," said the boy, pointing to a small, haphazardly constructed
shack. Flies buzzed noisily around it.

"That's the privy."

Tony heard Caroline gasp.

"Errr…ladies first," he said.

Later, Tony and Caroline followed the boy into the first of the three long buildings. In the fore-room a narrow table sat on an otherwise bare floor. Bottles and clay vessels lined rough shelves and assorted tools and implements hung next to the door. The building appeared to have suffered fire damage at some point. A girl, looking to be six years old at the most, sat cross-legged on the floor drawing on a yellowed, wrinkled piece of paper with a shard of charcoal. The aroma of a hearty vegetable-based stew wafted in from the next room, making Tony suddenly realize exactly how long it had been since he had eaten.

Tony looked back and saw the Wolf King's horseman well on his way back to the main building. Caroline grabbed him by the shoulder and turned him around.

"Okay, what the exact…" she stopped, peering at the girl. "What exactly is going on here, Tony?" asked Caroline. "Shouldn't these people be talking like Shakespeare or something?"

"No. Even assuming this is England, people in the 11th Century didn't speak anything like modern English. Remember *Beowulf* in English Lit? It would probably be something closer to that."

The bespectacled boy wandered over to the little girl and skeptically studied her handiwork.

"But that's not all," continued Tony, "this is all just …wrong. It's not like real history. It's like some fantasy version of medieval history. The armor those horsemen were wearing, that longsword, that giant tapestry, it's all wrong for the 11th Century. That "Wolf King" is obviously not from this time. I think he created this place somehow."

"You mean we're in a world designed by a Dungeons and Dragons geek from the future?"

"Something like that. But how big is this world?"

"Not that big," answered the boy, returning his attention to Tony and Caroline.

"What do you know of this place?" Tony asked him. "Where did you come from?"

"Highbury, Islington. I've been here for nearly a year now, I reckon. You lot are Yanks, aren't you? I visited my Auntie in Boston once, in the summer of '33. You talk like Yanks."

"We're from Texas," said Tony.

"You have oil wells in your backyards then?"

"Not me. You, Caroline?"

"Did Gaudet bring you here?" asked Caroline.

"No. It was another man who came to our school. Tall, dodgy looking fellow, handlebar moustache and beard, tatty Edwardian outfit, old. His name was John or Johann something, going by what I've heard. He said he would pay us fifteen bob a head to pick flowers in the country. He helped us sneak out. But the next thing we knew we were in some Flash Gordon car and here we were."

"Virge! Virgil, come and make yourself useful," called a woman's voice from the next room. A second later a short, grey haired woman stepped in. She wore a white apron over a faded sky-blue dress.

"Well, hello," she greeted them, a look of puzzlement and concern on her face.

"Hello. I'm Tony. This is Caroline. We're new here, I guess."

"Oh, you poor dears. You must be so scared and confused."

"Well..." began Tony.

"Yeah," said Caroline.

"I'm Wen," said the woman. "This is Virge," she continued, nodding at the boy, who now sat sullenly at the table. "And that," Wen added, indicating the little girl, "is our little angel Monique."

"She's dumb," said Virge.

"Don't say that, boy!"

"Well it's true. Won't say a word."

Caroline walked over to the girl.

"Oh, did you do that? That's so good! Look at what she drew!"

Monique had sketched a detailed portrait of Wen on the yellowed paper.

"Isn't that just precious," said Wen, stroking Monique's dark tresses. Monique looked up and smiled at Caroline.

"She likes you," said Wen.

She sighed.

"I expect the others will be getting back soon. Sit down, dears! I'll set two more places for dinner. Virge! Come help, boy!"

Over the course of the next few days, Tony and Caroline met the other workers who shared their living quarters or who lived in the adjoining barracks for servants. They were an odd assortment, plucked from locations all over world and from various periods, from the early 19th Century to the mid-21st Century, A.D. All spoke English, though for some it was a second or third language. As far as Tony could tell, no one on the castle grounds was native to the 11th Century. Most had not been there longer than two years.

Wen presented Tony with a new set of plain work clothes, and Caroline with a long, modest woolen dress. From daybreak until late each day they were set to various tasks inside the gates, mainly tending the livestock while being supervised by the Wolf King's men. After a couple of weeks, Tony and Caroline had almost gotten used to the routine, despite the long hours, uncomfortable cots they were given to sleep on, and the chill that crept in during the night through the cracks in the walls of their living quarters.

On the sixteenth day since being taken captive, Tony and several other men were led outside the gates of Selwys Castle to work in the fields beyond the land bridge. They spent a good portion of the day harvesting potatoes.

"You're lucky you didn't come in planting season," said Klemens, a servant who shared Tony's living quarters, "pulling a plow is back-breaking work."

Klemens was powerfully built for an older man, and he sported a trim grey moustache. His dark eyes seemed to always avoid the direct gaze of anyone he was speaking to.

A worn hoe was issued to Tony. He turned to the nearest mound in the field where the desiccated remains of the potato bush protruded and began hacking at the ground in a chopping motion.

"Anthony! We are not digging latrines here!" admonished Klemens. He grabbed the hoe.

"Just loosen the dirt, like this. Then reach down and gently pull out the potatoes. We do not want to damage them."

By the time they had trudged back to the castle grounds in the waning hours of the day, Tony's back was sore from bending over and his hands were raw from pulling tubers from the ground. As they were led back over the bridge, the supervising guard raised his hand to his mouth and said, "Gate." The outer gate parted to admit them. Tony could see no men working to draw it open.

Later, as they sat around the table for their evening meal, Tony decided that he could no longer keep the questions filling his head to himself.

"So," he began after awkwardly clearing his throat, "Virge was telling me the other day that this "kingdom" isn't very big. Has anyone ever been outside of it since getting here? Are there borders, or what?"

Caroline's eyes lit up in interest. Wen glanced towards the window nervously.

"There's something on the borders. Something that keeps outsiders from nosing about," answered Virge, still gnawing on a bit of chicken bone.

"I've been to the Mongrahan Hills beyond the land bridge," said Gil, a gangly boy of Tony's age who hailed from mid-21st Century Belgium. "We were looking for wild berries. It was clear from the way the guards were warning us that we were near one of the border areas. That's only about twenty five kilometers away."

"Mr. Sagret told me he had been all along the borders on a hunt with Wolfie's goons. He said they were rubbish hunters," scoffed Virge. "They didn't go far into the southern forest. It's like they were afraid themselves."

"How about to the east?" asked Caroline.

"The bay, and then beyond that, the sea," replied Gil.

"Do they take the servants fishing?"

"Never."

"Anyone ever head out that way?"

"You do not want to go that way," said Klemens sternly.

"Why not?"

"There are...dangers. Things. Things the Wolf King has created through twisted science. You do not want to encounter them."

"He said something about a dragon when he caught us. There was a man who escaped..."

"Farlowe," said Gil with a look of regret.

"So the dragon is real?" asked Tony. "Have any of you seen it?"

"The Drake is real," answered Klemens. "I have not seen it, thank the Almighty. But I have heard it. I have...smelled it. I have witnessed the Wolf King's minions feeding it through a door in the ground. It lives beneath the castle grounds in some unholy dungeon."

"Do any people live outside of the castle grounds?" asked Caroline. "Didn't he say something about other people, Tony?"

"Oh yeah, what was that?" Tony searched his memory. "Like he was deciding which group we should be assigned to."

"There are other people outside," said Wen. "They have their own village. That's what we've heard, at least."

"They keep to themselves," continued Gil. "Sometimes we see a strange face come through the gates, in a wagon drawn by horses. We are not allowed contact with the outsiders."

"What about the gate?" asked Tony. "How is it operated?"

"No more questions!" shouted Klemens, pounding the table. "I do not want trouble. You saw what happened to Farlowe."

"Klemens," said Wen, putting her hand on his. "They mean no harm. They're just curious."

"They will bring the wrath of the Wolf King upon us if they continue to ask these "harmless" questions. Have you not heard, Anthony? There is no escape. Why would you even want to escape? This is not a bad life."

"I've heard stories from the other workers. People being taken by wolves while watching livestock..." began Tony.

"Stories! I could tell you stories, boy. I was on the Italian front in the infantry of the Austro-Hungarian Empire during the Great War. I have seen boys barely old enough to shave buried in the mud of the trenches. Have you ever seen what mustard gas does to a person? You children would be crying and pleading for your mothers if you had seen half of the horrors I have witnessed. Here, we have a roof over our heads. We have food. If someone takes ill, the Wolf King provides medicine. All we have to do is tend his beasts and crops. It is an honest living. I will hear no more."

⋙ 10 ⋘

Estrella nervously glanced at the window again. Why did Isidoro not come? She had sent out Iaco, the houseboy, an hour ago. Behind her, Luna fretted at the table.

"Oh my soul," she said, exasperated. "Eat while the food is still hot and the milk still good."

But the child would not.

Isodoro would be sullen and quiet tonight, Estrella thought to herself, as her husband often was the night after an argument. Estrella felt that Isodoro had clearly overreacted. Her friendship with the young tailor was just that -- a harmless diversion and nothing more. It did get lonely in the house with no one to speak to but Luna and the houseboy. The trader's gossiping wife could be intolerable with her constant bird-like chatter.

She heard a commotion in the distance; voices raised, crying out in alarm. What was happening?

She opened the door and stepped down into the street. The air was dry. A scent of olives wafted from a neighbor's window. She was about to rouse the neighbors when she saw the houseboy running down the street, all color drained from his face.

"What has happened?" Estrella demanded when he reached her.

"It is terrible" Iaco said, gasping for breath. "A great angry mob is coming to the *Juderia*. They have killed the constable of *Jaén*!"

"Oh, Dear God!"

A church bell started pealing, raising the alarm.

"Where is Isidoro? Have you seen my husband?"

The boy shook his head.

"Why are they coming?"

"I think they mean to kill us all."

"But we converted years ago! Can nothing save us?"

"The old trader is telling us to hide indoors."

"I must find Isidoro. I will look for him at the shop."

"It is too late, Madame. They are here. I must get to my own family."

Estrella could hear angry shouting and horrified screams in the distance, coming ever closer.

"Stay here with Luna. I must find my husband. Do not let her leave your sight."

Estrella did not wait for the boy to answer. She ran down a back alley, away from the frightening clamor. With any luck, she could reach the glass shop where Isidoro was doubtlessly working away, oblivious, and bring him back to the house. Then they would decide whether to hole up or flee the oncoming storm of maddened humanity. Maybe the mob would not even turn down their street.

The houseboy looked after Estrella for half a minute. He trotted up the steps and looked through the open door at Luna, still sitting and playing with her food. She quizzically returned his glance.

"May God have mercy upon all of our souls," he said, closing the door and running away.

Luna got up from the table as the sounds from outside grew louder. She heard a horse galloping down the cobblestones in front of their house. Minutes later, she heard approaching footsteps. A tall man she had never seen before entered and closed the door behind him. He carried a twin-pronged staff and spoke in an odd accent.

"Don't be afraid," he said, but Luna was not frightened so much as puzzled.

"Make no sound. There are unfriendly people out there."

He took Luna by the hand and led her to a wardrobe.

"Hide inside there," the man instructed her.

He closed the door of the wardrobe and she sat in darkness. The shouts and screams from outdoors now sounded as if they were just beyond the doors of the wardrobe. She heard one word repeated, shouted by many angry voices: *Marranos*.

Finally there was a terrible crash that made her cry out in terror. There were sounds of a struggle and of furniture breaking and pots and dishes being flung about. Then it was quiet. She waited within the wardrobe, afraid to move.

The door opened and the strange man gently called for her to come out.

Another man lay on the floor next to the table, the remains of Luna's meal deposited on his head. His arms and legs twitched but he was clearly senseless.

"We must leave this place. I have a ship that can take us far from here."

The strange man stood by the door, listening. Outside, the sounds of human calamity seemed to be dying down. Luna stood her ground, but the man seized her by the hand and led her out the front door, down the steps and into the street. Outside, all along the *Juderia*, flames leapt out of windows. Doors were smashed in. Luna saw two familiar figures sprawled in the middle of the street beside some smashed flowerpots.

"Mama!" she cried.

"Don't look child! There is nothing we can do for her now."

He pulled Luna away.

"Why have these people done these things? Why do they call us such names?"

"If I live to see one thousand years of history, I will never understand it," replied the man.

ↂↂↂ

On the third week since his arrival, Tony was assigned to a new work group that included Caroline and Gil. They were given tasks within Selwys Castle grounds, including collecting eggs from the poultry coops and feeding livestock. Tony resigned himself to the labor without complaint, not wanting to incur the ire of the Wolf King's men. Today they were being supervised by Gerard, who was less tolerant of perceived laziness. Tony set himself to work carrying bundles of straw to the stables.

"Good day to you, Tony," said Daisy, leading a mare out of a stall. The horse was a gorgeous creature, with dark brown fur and a white streak on its forehead, seeming to form a cowl over its deep, intelligent eyes.

"Hello there, Daisy."

Daisy was a freckly-faced Australian girl from one of the neighboring workers' barracks.

"Psst, Tony! She likes you!" teased Caroline, who was helping with the straw bundles.

Tony glanced back at Daisy, who also turned and smiled. Tony quickly looked away.

"Your face is literally turning red! I've never seen anyone blush like that in my life!"

"The sun is getting to me."

"Yeah, it's the sun I'm sure," Caroline said sarcastically. "She is cute."

"Yes. She is."

"Get back to work, you two," growled Gerard.

Caroline made a face when Gerard looked away.

"I swear, one of these days," she began.

"Don't."

Tony dropped off the bundles he was lugging under each arm and returned to the pile. The bundles were stacked six feet high against an inner wooden fence that enclosed a small courtyard planted with bottle gentian and other colorful wildflowers. Tony pulled the top two bundles off the pile, and realized with a start that someone was standing just on the other side of the fence. It was the young woman known as Neon Sparrow. She smiled in a manner that Tony didn't find altogether friendly.

"Well, it's the new kid in town, as I live and breathe," she said in a faintly mocking tone.

Tony didn't know what to say so he just stood there, holding his tongue.

"That was pretty daring of you back there, telling Wolfie off like that." Her tone indicated a measure of actual respect. A hardness returned to her gaze.

"You'd better be careful around here, though. Those lances the guards carry aren't just for show."

"I've seen those before," said Tony, surprising himself with his bluster. "In a gaming arcade on the Time Station."

"Oh yeah?" replied Neon Sparrow, "well, these aren't like the ones in the holo-games. If they connect right, they could put you in a wheelchair for life. This is no game. And I wouldn't get on Wolfie's bad side either. He has an insane temper and never forgets a bad turn. He had me on ignore for a whole month last year just for some comments I made about his stupid sigil. Constructive criticism, of course."

Tony remained silent, feeling like an insect pinned to a collector's journal.

"My advice is: keep out of his way. Consider this a friendly warning."

"Boy! Get back to work," called Gerard.

Neon Sparrow turned her head in a dismissive gesture. Tony gathered up his bundles and turned back to the stables. As he walked back he noticed a guard trudge out of the booth near the gate and slowly limp along the fence.

The castle servants were let off from work earlier than usual that day. As soon as they got back to their barracks, Wen set Tony and Caroline to work peeling potatoes in the storage room adjacent to the kitchen area.

"I think I'm getting sick of these things," Caroline complained, crinkling her nose. "Every day it's potato stew or fish and chips, or mashed potatoes!"

"Potatoes aren't even supposed to exist in Eleventh Century Europe," answered Tony. "Spanish sailors brought them back from the New World during the age of the exploration."

"Did you learn that in Mrs. Livingston's history class?"

"No. I read it on a *Lord of the Rings* discussion board."

"Nerd. Well lucky for us then that...ow!"

"What's wrong? Did you cut yourself?"

"It's nothing," said Caroline. "I just have to stop for a bit." She dropped her potato paring knife and her arms fell to her sides.

"It's okay. I got it."

"Thanks, Tony. You're sweet."

Virge walked in, grabbed an armful of peeled potatoes, and walked out without a word. From the kitchen drifted the gamey odor of boiling venison.

"You know, this is just weird," said Caroline. "I mean…here we are! The Eleventh Century! Abducted by Renaissance Fair freaks from the future! We've been taking this in stride, but sometimes I think I'm going crazy!"

"I know what you mean. I think it's because we haven't had a chance to *think* about any of it. Everything has happened so fast since we got on that bus."

"It seems so long ago now. I always wanted to go somewhere, out of Texas. It just seems so…empty sometimes. You know that highway that goes out to Victoria, where my Dad used to live? It's just miles and miles of nothing. When you see a building it's abandoned. Like people tried living there once and then gave up."

Caroline sighed.

"Remember when you used to come over to my house in the summer? We'd watch t.v. in my room, then go out and play Power Rangers in the yard. And there was that house across the street with the old rusting tractor just sitting there, year after year."

"Yeah."

"There were times that I would have given anything to just make that thing disappear. It became this symbol to me. Something that just told me: *You are here. forever, with me. This is your life.* You know what I mean?"

"Yeah," replied Tony, "I think I know what you mean. I used to have these dreams. Like of places I'd never been, yet seemed familiar."

"I used to have this weird fantasy, or image in my head when I was young. I was living in this big old-fashioned city on a seashore, with houses all piled up on top of each other, built right up on a giant pier. And every day the fishermen would return with their catch, and I would bring them a big plate of food."

She chuckled.

"So you're a waitress in your fantasy?"

Caroline flicked a potato peeling at Tony. "No! I'm just bringing them food because I'm a nice person and I'm appreciative of the hard work they're doing."

Hunter, a pet grey tabby wandered in and slinked against Caroline's leg. Caroline reached down and scratched him around his ears.

"I miss my Bosco. And my Ipod, my computer, my bed, and my Beatles records."

"You like The Beatles? I thought you were all emo now?"

"So I can't like The Beatles because I like to wear black now? Tony, you are funny sometimes."

"Okay, what's your favorite Beatles song?"

"It's "Hello, Goodbye." What's yours?"

"Mine is "A Hard Day's Night," I guess. My Dad used to play it with his rock band."

"Get out! Your Dad was in a rock band?"

"Yeah, they used to play all over south Texas back in the day. He was the guitarist. The other guys in the band would come over to the house and jam when I was little. I still remember my Dad playing that one."

"What were they called?"

"Rene and the Rockeros. We have a picture in the garage of them standing in front of some biker bar in the Valley. They're all crossing their arms and scowling. When I was a kid I always wondered why they looked so mad in the picture." Tony laughed at the memory.

"So what happened to the band?"

"I don't know. They never took off, I suppose. Then Dad inherited the family hardware store, and he couldn't spend all his time on the road anymore."

"Is that the plan for you?"

"I guess. I don't know. We don't talk much about it, I suppose."

"You guess? Great Caesar's Ghost, Tony! You don't talk much with your Dad about your life?"

"Well, yeah. No. I don't know."

Tony shrugged.

"Sometimes, Tony, I just don't know what to think of you."

Caroline shook her head.

"Oh, you know what, Tony? I almost forgot to tell you!"

"What?"

"I was talking to Monique the other day and she said some interesting things!"

"Wait. Run that back? You were talking to her? I thought she didn't speak?"

"She does talk! In Spanish! Well, it's like Spanish, but an old-fashioned dialect or something. Maybe she's from Spain."

"Did she say? How did she get here anyways?"

"She told me that she lived in a town near some mountains. One day, some people came and set fire to her neighborhood and killed her parents. Then Gaudet came and hid her until they left, and then brought her here."

"Well, at least he's not completely evil."

"Yeah, but of all places to take her…"

"Uh huh,"

"But that's not the most interesting part. She told me that she saw one of the Wolf King's men opening the gate last week."

"Seriously?"

"No one was paying attention and she walked all the way to that booth next to the gate. She said there was a machine there – a computer I guess, or a keypad. There were workers returning from the fields. The guy in the booth pressed some keys, and the gate opened. Then he turned around and saw her and brought her back here."

"Wow. A bit of a security breach, there."

"Yeah, but probably not one they're worried about, because she's just a little girl who doesn't even talk –- as far as they know."

"Hmm. And maybe that guard wouldn't *want* to report it, because it would make him look like a screw-up in front of the Wolf King. Did she get a good look at the keys he pressed?"

"She must have. She was right behind him."

"Oh, but she probably doesn't know letters and numbers, does she?"

Caroline frowned and furrowed her brow. "I don't think she does."

They fell silent for a moment.

"You know what? I just got a crazy idea," said Tony. "Monique might not have been taught, but she has a good eye for detail. Can you bring her in here?"

"Okay." Caroline walked out and returned leading Monique in by her hand. She walked up to Tony with a smile.

"Oh, look at that pretty flower in her hair," cooed Caroline.

"Hello, Monique," said Tony. "My Spanish is pretty rusty. Can you help me out, Caroline?"

"I think she understands English. She just doesn't speak it."

Tony gently took Monique's hands in his own.

"Monique, do you remember when you were at the booth by the gate? Gate...uh...*la portilla*?" He pointed in the direction of the gate and booth.

Monique nodded.

"You saw the man press the buttons? *Recuerdas el hombre pulsando los botones?*"

She nodded again.

"Can you *draw* what you saw on the buttons he pressed? *Puedes dibujar ...los botones?*"

Tony picked up a handful of sawdust from a table in the corner and spread it on the floor. He ran his finger through it once to make sure she understood, and then spread the sawdust evenly across the floor again.

Monique frowned in concentration. She then kneeled down and traced in the sawdust, "3 – 1 – 3."

⊰⊱ 11 ⊰⊱

T wo days passed before Tony had another chance to talk to Caroline privately, when they were assigned the task of husking corn in a storage shed.

"Are you sure we want to do this?"

"I've never been more sure," answered Caroline.

"Should we take anyone? Virge?"

"He's too young and small. And what if he breaks or loses his glasses?"

"Wen?"

"I doubt if she could keep up."

"Klemens?"

They looked at each other and said, "No," simultaneously, laughing.

"Do you even believe that bit about him being a soldier in World War I?" asked Tony. "I heard him singing something by Iron Maiden once when we were working in the fields."

"He could have picked it up from someone here."

Tony shrugged.

"Anyway, how do *you* know Iron Maiden? I thought you were all "nerd" now."

"Very funny! My Dad actually took me to a concert by them once when I was around nine. It was his idea of a bonding experience, I guess."

"Oh, fun."

"Actually, it was," replied Tony soberly.

Klemens could be heard outside, boisterously belting out a chorus from "Rigoletto" as he repaired an animal pen that had collapsed during a recent heavy rainstorm. Caroline giggled.

"We probably have a better chance of sneaking out if it's just the two of us," continued Tony. "Anyway, I don't want anyone else to risk their life. Once we get beyond the, um, temporal stasis field they must have to keep everyone here, we'll have to be prepared to be "swooped," hopefully back to our time."

"How do we know how far to go, though?"

"It makes sense that if we reach the borders, we'll be beyond the stasis field. In fact, the borders probably are the limits of the field. That's why the Wolf King's men were afraid to go too far into the forests south of Selwys Castle."

"So Karlo is on guard duty tonight?"

"If they follow the regular rotation. We can get within roughly twenty yards of the booth if we keep low and use the pens, fences, and storage shacks for cover. Then we wait. I've been watching Karlo during his daytime shifts. He walks back and forth along the fence, between the booth and guard barracks. Towards the end of his shift, he gets slower and slower. At the end of his shift he makes one final trip from the booth to the barracks, walks halfway back to the booth, then stops and returns to the barracks to get the guy who relieves him on guard duty.

"So we make for the booth when he starts walking back to the barracks…"

"And then we get maybe another minute-and-a-half or so to figure out how to open the gate."

"And if we can't figure it out? Or if they've changed the code?"

"Then, *maybe* we have time to run back to cover before Karlo's relief shows up. It's a gamble."

"I'm ready," said Caroline.

That night, Tony lay awake in his cot, not daring to even momentarily close his eyes. The castle bell tolled a quarter 'til two o'clock. He got up as quietly as possible and stepped into the narrow hallway. Caroline appeared half a minute later, emerging from the women's quarters on the other side of the hall. Tony nodded at her wordlessly. Together, they crept to the end of the building, where Tony cautiously cracked the rear door. Just as they stepped out, Tony heard a creaking sound behind them. They turned. Monique stood at the door.

"No, go back, Monique," said Caroline. *"Regresamos."*

Monique frowned and fretted but finally went back inside.

Keeping low, Tony and Caroline dashed between pens and stables in the cool night air until they reached the storage shed nearest the booth at the outer gate. Crouching down there, they could see Karlo limping along the outer fence in the light of the waning gibbous moon.

"How can we tell when he is going for his relief?" whispered Caroline.

"He'll bring his mug back with him."

They waited and watched as Karlo made three more halting trips between the booth and guard barracks. Tony imagined he could hear Karlo's labored breathing as he trudged along. Karlo stepped into the booth and then emerged a minute later.

"Is that...? Yes, he's got the mug," said Tony. "Get ready."

Karlo was about halfway to the barracks when Tony whispered, "Go!"

He sprinted towards the booth. Caroline's steps thumped on the ground just behind him but didn't look back. They entered the booth.

"He still hasn't reached the barracks yet," observed Caroline, looking back.

"Duck," warned Tony, crouching down.

The booth was empty save for a stool and a small table. On the wall nearest the outer gate was mounted a keyboard pad with numbers and symbols.

"Do it, Tony," prompted Caroline.

Tony took a deep breath and punched 3 and 1 and 3 again. Nothing happened. He shot a panicked look at Caroline.

"Try it again."

Tony entered the same sequence of numbers, but still the gate remained in place. He tried punching in the numbers in different sequences.

"Oh God, he's starting to come back!" warned Caroline, peeking through a crack in the boards.

"We're going to have to make a break for the storage shed when he turns around again."

"It doesn't look like he's turning! Did he forget something here?"

Tony's blood froze when he noticed Karlo's Wolf insignia cloak hanging from a nail in the wall.

Just then a familiar voice shouted.

"Karlo, you game-legged goose-stepper! Has stamping on the dreams of helpless people made you lame?"

"Klemens, you fool. Go back to your barracks. It is long past curfew. I am in no mood for your drunken ranting tonight."

Tony turned to Caroline. "He's got Karlo's attention. But if he keeps it up, he'll wake up every guard on the Castle grounds. We've got to go back."

"Yeah, I suppose so," said Caroline with some regret. She took another look at the keyboard pad.

"Wait! What if it is 3 *slash* 3?"

Without hesitating, Tony punched in 3 / 3. There was a mechanical whirring sound as the machinery came to life and the gate began to draw open.

"We did it! Let's make a break for it while we can!"

Karlo and Klemens were still arguing as they exited the booth. Tony looked back. Karlo had finally noticed the activity at the gate. Klemens grabbed Karlo by the arm, turning him back around, and punched him square on the chin. Karlo crashed to the muddy earth like a felled tree. Klemens pointed to the gate and mouthed, "Run."

Tony turned and followed Caroline out of the front gate just before it closed behind them.

"This way," said Tony.

They fled over the bridge, hopped a small outer fence and ran along the coast of the peninsula, not pausing until they had crossed the land bridge. From there they headed in a southwest direction, sticking to the margins of the marshlands.

"I have to rest, Tony," gasped Caroline.

"We can't rest for too long."

Tony looked back in the direction of Selwys Castle. Tiny points of light appeared in the distance.

"Oh no. Not good."

"What do we do, Tony?"

"We've got to split up."

"No."

"It will double the chance that one of gets through. If you make it and I don't, you send help somehow. Find Mr. Marinos at the beach."

"You send help for me, buddy."

"I think we're pretty close to the place we first arrived. You keep going that way -- west -- and you'll reach the Meddywyn, that small river we saw. Gil said there are places you can wade across. Swim if you have to, but watch the current. If they have a dog that should throw the scent off. Once beyond it, just keep going. You'll reach the border eventually."

"And what's your plan, bright guy?"

"I'll head straight south and try to loose them in the forest. Eventually I'll make it beyond the stasis field. Are you alright, Caroline?"

"Just catching my breath."

He squeezed Caroline's hand.

"Okay. Let's go!"

Caroline sprinted towards the Meddywyn.

Tony watched her for a minute and then headed towards the thickening growth of trees that marked the outskirts of the Southern Forest. He tripped on a root and sprawled face forward into the damp, leaf covered ground. He leapt up and continued running. There were no sounds of pursuit. He tried to navigate using the stars, but it was too overcast to make out any familiar constellations.

Before long Tony admitted to himself that he was completely lost. He splashed through a small brook and trotted in the direction his best estimate told him was south. After hiking for another couple of hours, he collapsed to the ground under a gnarled oak, too exhausted to continue. He was momentarily startled by a loon's call. The waterfowl's mournful cry made him shiver in spite of himself. Tony closed his eyes.

He awoke with a start. The sun had risen, but he was chilled to the bone. After stiffly rising to his feet, Tony surveyed his surroundings. All was seemingly calm, but he still could not place where he was in relation to any of the geographic landmarks he was familiar with.

He calculated that he must be somewhere in the main expanse of the Southern Forest now, miles to the south and west of the clearing where Gaudet had originally brought them in his shuttle. He pulled a piece of Wen's corn bread out of his pocket and ate half of it, saving the uneaten portion. Out of his other pocket he produced a strawberry and chewed it slowly, savoring the juice, as he was very thirsty by now. Tony had no other provisions.

Tony forlornly tried to convince himself that Caroline had also safely eluded the pursuit from the castle. He hiked towards a lone hill jutting out of the trees ahead, hoping that he could spot a recognizable landmark from that vantage point. A sudden motion on the side of the hill caught his eye and Tony froze in his tracks and crouched down. There was no doubt about it. Someone was climbing down the side of the hill.

Tony turned and ran. He heard something that sounded like a war whoop. Something fell from above him, simultaneously tripping and blinding him. He felt his ankle twist. Tony fell in agony and despair.

❧ 12 ❧

Klemens was born in the year 1895 in a central district of the city of Zagreb to a once affluent family of declining fortunes. His brother Karlo was two years his senior, and clearly favored by their father Osvald, despite often being a source of embarrassment to the family. Osvald had, in feckless youth, frittered away most of what was left of the family fortune and married Jelena, a poor girl he found singing with a *tamburitza* orchestra in Vojvodina. Klemens inherited Jelena's love of music but found the works for piano of Liszt and Smetana and Wagner's Ring Cycle more revelatory than any folk or Gypsy song.

Osvald tried his best to convince his sons that service in the military was a sound career choice. Klemens had some reservations with increased Russian aggression and the specter of war falling as a dread shadow over the Balkans, but no alternatives immediately presented themselves. Osvald still had enough influence to have Klemens and Karlo enrolled in an officer training program. In June of 1914, Klemens accepted an officer's commission in the army of the Austro-Hungarian Empire. Two weeks later, the Archduke of the Empire, Franz Ferdinand, was assassinated by Serbian nationalist Gavrilo Princip, plunging the world into conflagration.

Klemens' unit was assigned to the Italian front. Fighting was fierce, and soon Klemens could remember nothing aside from the smoke, mud, and metal of a gray world at war. After several months, Klemens received word that Karlo had been injured in battle on the Russian Front and discharged from the army.

Back at the Italian front, Klemens performed his duties efficiently, but on one fateful occasion, when his unit received orders to advance, Klemens froze. His batman prodded, cajoled, and cursed him, but he would not budge. Klemens, for his part, was aware on some level of his batman shaking him by the shoulders and screaming in his face, but Klemens was far away, in a land untroubled by explosions, flamethrowers, poison gas, and roaring motors. He was in a fantastic country of verdant forests and swift sparkling streams, populated by giants, Rhine maidens, dragons, dwarfs and Valkyries sailing across a cerulean firmament astride winged stallions.

Ultimately, the batman was able to guide Klemens to his feet, while basically taking command of the situation and guiding the troops' advance into enemy lines. Not a word was spoken about it afterward. It was as if it had never happened. The battle was deemed a great victory for the Empire, and Klemens was decorated by his superiors.

When the Great War ended, Klemens returned to his home in Zagreb, where Karlo now lived with Jelena. Osvald had managed to drink himself to death during the wartime years. Klemens and Karlo formed a social club of veterans of the Great War, which would meet on a monthly basis at a local tavern. At first the meetings proved cathartic and healing. As the years passed, personal and political differences between certain members arose, not the least between Klemens and Karlo, and meetings were often marked with acrimony or sullen formality replacing camaraderie as memories of the war receded into the past. Eventually, the club was no more than a group of middle-aged men, returning by habit to stare across the table at increasingly unfriendly faces.

Karlo, for his part, had now become increasingly supportive of the nationalist movement in Croatia, and drew inspiration from the Austrian-born political agitator Hitler. Jelena died heartbroken. Klemens, now working in a low-level government position, pondered his next move as the specter of total war engulfed the globe again.

It was at this time that the man who identified himself only as Johannes appeared. He approached Klemens and Karlo following one of the final, desultory meetings of the veterans' club. Johannes claimed to have seen the future and what he foretold for the Balkans unsettled both brothers: years of unrelenting world war giving way to

Communist rule, threat of nuclear annihilation, chaos, upheaval, and ethnic cleansing. Johannes' offer was quite simple: he would take both brothers away to an idyllic country, untroubled by modern warfare. They would be placed in positions of authority, as befitting former officers of a great Empire. After ten years of service, they would be returned to any nation of their choosing, rich men for their troubles. In the new land, Klemens dove into his new role with the mechanical efficiency he had adopted to survive his tenure at the Italian front. But as the years passed, Klemens became convinced that there would never be a return trip for him.

eⒼⓊ

After leaving Tony, Caroline continued to skirt the edge of the marshlands until she spotted the Meddywyn, its languid stream glinting in intermittent moonlight. It was difficult to discern how deep it was in the darkness; she wasn't sure she would have been able to tell even in the daylight. Caroline followed its banks southward. Finally, when some jagged rocks appeared protruding from the water, she decided to take her chances. The water was shockingly cold as she stepped in, but only rose slightly above knee-level. The rocks were too uneven to use as stepping stones, but with some difficulty she was able to wade across the slippery bottom of the stream, lifting the hem of her dress with one hand and grabbing onto the rocks with her other hand for support. She headed for cover of the trees on the far side and continued in a southwesterly direction, striving to keep the stream within sight.

As Caroline continued, the path of the Meddywyn diverged increasingly from the line of trees. She was reluctant to leave the cover they provided, so she jogged under the branches of the trees as the stream receded in the distance. After about an hour of hiking she found herself walking along the edge of a rocky ravine that looked like it might have been an old bed for the Meddywyn. It seemed the least obstructed path, so she continued following it.

Suddenly there was a blur of motion at her feet. Caroline yelled in surprise, lost her footing and tumbled down the side of the ravine. She felt rough rocks and scrub tearing at her clothes and skin as she tumbled and then a sharp pain in her left calf and a horrible jolt as she came to rest at the bottom.

Caroline lay still for several seconds. Gingerly, she moved and tested her extremities. She had taken a blow to the back of her head, a painful jolt to her right elbow, and was scratched all over. Worst of all, there was an alarming crooked gash on her left calf. In near shock, she saw her own blood glistening in the moonlight as it exited the wound. Caroline found the place where the rock shard had perforated her dress, stuck her fingers through it, and began tearing the cloth. When she had a long enough strip from the hem of her dress, she cleaned the wound as best as she could, applied pressure to it, and then bandaged it as tightly as possible, tightening it with a ribbon she had been using to pull her hair back into a ponytail. She lay on her back on the cold ground for several minutes, feeling faint. She raised her wounded leg and rested it on a rock. There was no possibility of looking for cover at the moment; it would have been physically impossible.

After resting for about half an hour, Caroline began to feel her strength returning, although she still felt great pain. Nearby she spotted an old burlap sack caught in a bush. With difficulty, she rose to her feet and extricated it. Using a sharp rock she cut it along one side, unfolding it into one roughly four-foot length of cloth. With her remaining strength she stumbled to a grassy area behind the bush growth and collapsed to the ground, covering herself as best as she could with the burlap. She soon fell into exhausted sleep.

The sun had risen into the hazy morning sky when Caroline awoke. Her left leg was very sore below the knee. She checked the bandage, examined her wound, and then tied it up again. She decided to risk continuing. The ravine was too steep to climb out of in her current state so she limped along the bottom at the best speed she could manage. Eventually, the ravine grew more shallow and Caroline was able to stumble up the right bank. She could not see or hear the Meddywyn anymore. Thick tree and brush growth extended on both sides. The only open path appeared to be along the edge of the ravine.

Caroline rested for a while and snacked on some strawberries she had stored in a pouch in her dress. She had just started hobbling forward again when she heard a tremendous crash. In shock, she watched as a full sized buck deer sprang out of the thicket directly in her path.

She stumbled back, off balance. The buck landed, took several steps and then turned around, facing Caroline, its eyes dark and menacing. It raised its hackles and lowered its horns.

"Oh, you've got to be kidding," said Caroline to herself. She noticed something sticking out of the buck's flank, as she frantically looked for cover.

The buck snorted and charged. Caroline could do nothing but fall to the ground and cover her face. She heard the deer grunt and then stop. She opened her eyes and saw a woman with a short archer's recursive bow poised on an outcropping of rock ahead. The buck now had two arrows protruding from its flank. A third arrow was notched and loosed by the woman. It found its target, and the deer stumbled and collapsed to the ground.

"Wow," gasped Caroline.

The woman scrambled down from the rock, calling out and reaching Caroline's side in seconds.

"Oh, you're hurt," she said. She had long white hair and wore brown and green fringed clothing that blended into the forest background. She possessed a hard beauty, as if her high cheekbones, pointed chin and Roman nose had been shaped by the untamed elements as sandstone carved by wind and rain over the course of centuries. The woman took Caroline's hand, as if to reassure her, then examined her leg.

"You shouldn't be walking on that."

"Please, can you help me? I got separated from my friend. We're lost here."

A second stranger emerged the brush. He had thick curly hair, Mediterranean features and was dressed in similar brown and green garb. He also carried a small bow and a full quiver of arrows.

"Garsen, help. This girl has been injured. We must take her back to the village."

"No!" pled Caroline. "Not to the castle! No, no..."

The woman's brow furrowed.

"Do not be troubled, girl. We will take you to our village of Calendenny. You will find rest and help there, as you need it. Fear no pursuit, if you are flying from the King's servants."

Before Caroline could utter another word of protest, the man called Garsen picked her up effortlessly and gently carried her. At that point,

Caroline could not have objected if she had wanted to. Weakness and numbness had overcome her again. In a growing haze she saw the tree growth thin out and a path through the forest materialize. Soon a wooden post fence and buildings appeared in a clearing ahead. Just as she was carried into a log house with a pointed roof, Caroline again slipped into unconsciousness.

Caroline awoke, finding herself resting on a comfortable white bed with a feather down pillow in a small room. Her wound had been dressed and re-bandaged. She felt better, but there was still an intermittent throbbing pain in her calf. She raised her head from her pillow and was met by the curious gaze of a girl sitting on a stool in the corner.

"Hello," the girl said. She had thick curled locks that cascaded over her shoulders and wore a pale yellow dress with brocades. Her eyes projected a gentle sense of private amusement.

"How are you feeling?"

Caroline sat up.

"Um, I think my leg's better now."

"Don't strain yourself. Vanaya says you must rest today. We'll have some soup for you in a bit. There is a privy outside if you need it."

"Oh, great. I mean, thanks," said Caroline, feeling a bit self-conscious. The girl continued to stare at her.

"My name is Tegwyn. What's yours?"

"My name is Caroline."

"That's a pretty name. I haven't heard that one before."

"Thank you. It was my Aunt's name."

Tegwyn nodded, although she appeared a bit puzzled.

"Is this your first time in Calendenny?"

"Huh? Oh. Yes. I've never been here."

"Where did you come from?"

"Far away. I'm a stranger here. Me and my friend are lost. Have you seen him? His name is Tony."

Tegwyn shook her head.

At that moment, the white haired woman opened a door and entered the room.

She walked up to Caroline and quickly inspected her wound.

"No sign of infection, thank the Good Mother," she said.

She put her hand on Caroline's forehead.

"Temperature is somewhat high. Best continue resting for now."

"My friend!" Caroline protested, "You've got to help my friend. He might be in trouble, too."

"Garsen and some others went looking for your friend. Which path did he take?"

"He was heading south, on the other side of the stream. The Meddywyn, I think it's called."

"You were fleeing the Wolf King's men."

Caroline froze.

"Do not fear. We will not give you to the King, even though we fear him. We can conceal you if his men come to our doors here in Calendenny."

"He knows about this place?"

"Certainly. We Elves often deal with the Wolf King."

"E...Elves?"

"Yes. We are Elves here in Calendenny."

The girl in the corner giggled, sensing Caroline's puzzlement.

"That is Tegwyn, my gift from the Good Mother."

"We've met," said Caroline, still wondering if some prank was being played on her.

"Tegwyn! Go fetch nourishment for our guest."

"Yes, Vanaya," said the girl, obediently. She ran out of the room and dutifully returned with a ceramic bowl filled nearly to the brim with soup. Little wisps of steam rose from it. Caroline took the wooden spoon Tegwyn offered her and ate, not stopping until she was sipping the broth.

"My, you were hungry!" laughed Vanaya. "I'll take it as a good sign that you still have a healthy appetite. Sleep now and we shall talk later. We shall have plenty of warning if the King's men approach. Rest."

❧ 13 ❧

C aroline drifted in and out of sleep. She was vaguely aware of a man entering the room, cleaning her wound again and applying some ointment, and changing the bandages. At one point she saw stars twinkling through the window. After what seemed like days later she woke to see sunlight streaming in, accompanied by a sweet scent, as of some exotic flowers she was unfamiliar with. The feverishness she had felt before had subsided. There were voices outside. She sat up, tested her weight, and found she could walk without much difficulty.

Tegwyn entered and smiled at her.

"Oh, you're up. Just in time for breakfast."

Caroline was seated at an oval shaped table in an adjoining room. Vanaya and Garsen were there, along with a man she had not met before. Tegwyn introduced him as Kinnemort. A hearty breakfast was set with scrambled eggs, ham, berries and milk.

Vanaya stood, took the hand of Garsen, and announced, "We give thanks to the Good Mother Endewyn who brought us to this world and taught us to walk in it."

She sat and they ate. Caroline was anxious for word of Tony, but no one spoke during the meal.

"Oh, I must have gotten your cup," apologized Caroline, noticing the ceramic mug she was drinking milk from.

"What's that?" asked Vanaya.

"This cup has your name on it. "Vanaya." And there's a picture of a little girl with black hair glazed on it. Was your hair dark when you were younger?"

"No, I was fair haired. The tribulations of life in Calendenny have turned my hair white long before my winter."

"Oh. Who made this cup? It's beautiful craftsmanship."

Vanaya gazed at Caroline blankly.

"That cup has always been here, since I was brought to this world by the Good Mother. As was this dwelling, and the entire village of Calendenny."

"I see. When were you brought to this world?"

"Many years ago when I was a little girl I was brought from the Other World. Garsen came shortly afterward, then the rest you see in this village."

"Other world? Oh, I see. What do you remember of the other world?"

"We all have vague memories," answered Kinnemort, "but they have faded, like dreams. Some of us remember cities of titans, with cyclopean, impossible buildings reaching into the sky."

"I remember the Vid. Magic windows that showed other lands and people," said Garsen. "And the...autos. Great metal engines that moved under their own power on big black wheels."

"I do not remember such things," said Vanaya. "I remember a world not too different from this one, except it was much colder and snowfall more frequent. I still recall the words of another language I once spoke in the Other World."

"When did the Wolf King bring you here?"

Vanaya raised her eyebrows.

"The Wolf King? He did not bring us here. The Good Mother brought us here."

"The Good Mother? I meant, like actually brought you here. From the Other World."

"That is what she meant," said Garsen.

"Oh, I thought "The Good Mother" was what -- who -- you call... God?"

"Endewyn is not believed to be of the gods. Most think she was of true Elf-kind. She had us brought here as children by her servants and she taught us the way of this world. We were taught how to farm, how to hunt, how to sew our own clothes, and all other necessary crafts."

"She taught us the way of Elves," continued Vanaya. "Our stories, our beliefs, how to use our faculties in harmony with this world."

"I see. So that was before the Wolf King came, then."

"The Wolf King has always been here," responded Vanaya. "I remember seeing him when I was a little girl. We have always paid him a tribute from our harvests."

"He's always been here? How long have you been here?"

"I have counted nearly thirty winters in this world."

"Wow. He didn't seem that old. He didn't look much older than Tony or me."

"He is a sorcerer, one who tampers with the natural order of the world, or so many believe. He does not age as humans and Elf-kind do."

"Did the Good Mother ever say where she came from? And where is she now?"

"She spoke sometimes of a land called Wales. I believe that is where she lived once. She and her servants left us after many years teaching us and protecting us."

"When did you last see her?"

"Eleven years past, in the waning days of autumn, she returned and brought me dear Tegwyn. She was just a babe in arms then. But the Good Mother told us that she could not tarry, and departed mysteriously, as she does."

Caroline pondered Vanaya's words. She noticed something glinting on the floor.

"Oh, someone must have dropped a spoon," she said, reaching down.

"Don't touch it!" cried Tegwyn.

"Okay," said Caroline, taken aback. She turned to the others at the table but they said nothing.

"Vanaya, you've been so kind in helping me out here. I mean you've been great. But I really need to find my friend. I'm so worried about him."

"Yes, we have not forgotten him, you can rest assured. However, we have been unable to locate him. It does not appear to us that the King's men followed him south, if that was indeed his path. We are investigating another lead today. Garsen and I will set out soon. Hopefully we will know something definite by the time we return this evening. Do not lose hope! Tegwyn will keep you company today. If some emergency arises, Kinnemort will be on hand to assist."

Vanaya and Garsen rose.

"Tegwyn! Put the plates and tableware away. And do be careful, angel."

Vanaya and Garsen left. Tegwyn gingerly removed the plates on the dining table and moved them to a roughly constructed counter on which sat a basin of water. She rinsed the dishes and wiped them off with a rag, humming to herself.

"So, are you going to pick up that spoon?" asked Caroline.

"Eh? No. It is no longer ours."

Caroline looked at the spoon doubtfully.

"Whose is it?"

"It belongs to the *Tylwyth Teg.*"

"The...what?"

"The *Tylwyth Teg.* You know. The good people."

Caroline returned a blank look.

"*Tylwyth Teg.* Fairies!"

"Fairies?" Caroline looked at the floor suspiciously.

"Yes. The spoon hit the floor, so it belongs to them."

"What if you drop your food on the floor?"

"Then it belongs to the cat. Or the dog, whichever is faster." She giggled.

"What if you drop money? Do you have money here?"

"Sometimes the King's men will give us small gold or copper coins in exchange for crops or other things, without the King's knowledge. Some in Calendenny think they are valuable and trade with them within the village. I have a penny that Carith gifted to me on the anniversary of my arrival. But if I should drop the penny on the floor, it would belong to the *Tylwyth Teg.*"

The day passed, and Tegwyn regaled Caroline with tales of fairies and their mysterious invisible world, the doings of the village Calendenny and rumors of the Kingdom around them. She briefly allowed Caroline outdoors while she drew water from the well. But Vanaya and Garsen did not return that day.

Caroline returned to her room early in the evening where Tegwyn kept her company and played a board game similar to chess with her. The pieces were hand carved of limewood in the likeness of fair looking knights, oddly stunted warriors, and proud kings. After several games, Caroline fell back on the bed, too tired to sit up.

"Where could they be?" she wondered aloud.

"Oh, you poor thing. You're still worried about your friend."

Tears began streaming down Caroline's face. She turned, suddenly self-conscious.

"There, there. Don't worry. Vanaya and Garsen are our best hunters and trackers. I'm sure they will find your friend and bring him back here safely."

"Oh, I hope so...please, please, I hope so."

Tegwyn wiped her tears with a cloth handkerchief.

"Here. I want you to have this." She held out a small brown coin. "Carith gave it to me, and now it's yours."

"Oh, that's sweet of you, Tegwyn."

"Just lie back and rest. Do you want to hear a story? It is a story that Vanaya told me that the Good Mother taught her in turn, years ago."

"Oh. Sure. I'd love to hear a good story."

Tegwyn clasped her hands in front of her and began reciting:

"Many years ago, there lived a Princess of a great kingdom. In this kingdom, the King's court was a place of wonder, beauty, and music. People came from distant lands just to see the spectacle of great murals and relief sculptures adorning the palace, skilled fire-eaters and tumblers, and marvelous music made by the musicians of the court. But the main attraction at every performance by the King's musicians was the Princess, named Celestine, for she was a skilled player of the lute. Her music created visions of faraway lands and things lost or forgotten. Her music gave people clarity of mind and connected ideas within their minds in ways that they had never before considered.

Princess Celestine loved to travel, and often set out to foreign lands in the company of stout men of the King's court. On one occasion during her travels, she chanced to come upon a small kingdom many leagues distant from her home. Within the borders of this land the Princess' party came upon a beautiful enclosed glade where she longed to tarry.

"But," said one of her company, "there is a dire warning written here at the gate that strangers may not enter."

Princess Celestine would not be dissuaded. Upon entering the gate, her company was waylaid by fierce soldiers of the kingdom. The Princess and her men bargained for their freedom and promised great ransom from their King, but the soldiers were unmoved and brought the Princess and her company before their own sovereign, King Edric.

"Who are you that have made this unsolicited incursion into our lands?" asked King Edric.

"That was only I," replied Princess Celestine, "Princess of a far-away but great kingdom, and my small company of men. But we only encroached on these lands and entered the glade in ignorance and meant no harm. We will be only too happy to set off and never return if you would be so gracious as to grant us leave, O Lord."

"It is death for outsiders who enter the sacred glade without permission. That is the law, set by my fathers. I am not happy for it, but there can be no exceptions."

"Then let me bear the punishment," replied the Princess. "For it was by my command that we have so encroached upon these lands."

"Very well," said King Edric. "Your men will not face death, but they may never again leave my kingdom."

That night Princess Celestine was given a final meal of her choosing and told to prepare for execution. When the fateful hour arrived, she suddenly cried out to King Edric, "Wait! There is something I must show you first."

She took her lute from her traveling bag and began playing a minstrel's song of her land. The music of the lute was unknown in this kingdom, and so enchanted was King Edric that he halted the execution, "For," said he, "I must have such beauteous music enrich my own royal court. But alas! I cannot circumvent the law of my fathers!"

"I propose this then," replied Celestine. "I will teach you how to play this instrument. When I have taught you all that I know, you may proceed with the sentence ordained by your fathers."

"I agree," replied King Edric.

"However, I must set one firm condition: I will only teach you and no one else in your court. For this lute is an instrument of royalty and it is not meet that one who does not sit upon a throne should learn the secrets of this music."

King Edric acquiesced. Thereafter, every day for twelve months Princess Celestine took Edric into a private chamber and taught him the art of the lute, the reading of scales, the tunings, and the many marvelous melodies of her own country. While she was not giving Edric music lessons, she was allowed to work on her own in the chambers of the King's craftsmen. She also spent many hours alone in her own chamber, always asking for ink and paper to write upon.

After a year and a day had passed, Celestine presented the King with a remarkable gift: a lute that she had built with her own hands out of wood from trees grown in the forests of King Edric's kingdom.

"And now," she said, "you have learned everything I can teach. But I ask one final boon before you pass doom upon me: You must accompany me in the performance of this piece of music I have written. It is my life's work, and I would hear it once before I go to my final reward."

The King was loath to finally execute the sentence of death he had long ago passed upon the Princess, and could hardly deny her last request.

"But," said he, "I have never seen music like this."

"This is your part," Celestine said, pointing to the notations on the papers she placed in front of them, "and this in lighter script is mine."

And so the King began playing Celestine's composition. He played an introductory theme. It was answered by Celestine on her own instrument. The theme repeated for several more bars and then Celestine began playing a counter-melody. Gentle finger-picked phrases Edric played were augmented by strumming by Celestine, and descending runs of triplets were answered by ascending sixteenth notes. Another querulous main theme began and was answered by an impatient counter-theme, whose notes seemed to fall into the gaps of the second main theme. For a time, it seemed as if the two lutes were dueling, arguing, and contesting each other. Then a final peaceful closing theme began. Now the lutes seemed no longer to be at odds, with Celestine's lute sadly agreeing with the solemn pronouncements of the final theme played by Edric, though occasionally adding its own thoughts. The final theme spoke of rivers that had flowed endlessly since the world was created, of people looking at the same stars in different corners of the world who would never meet, of dreams shared by men from the lowliest of peasants to the richest emperor on earth. When it ended, King Edric was in tears.

"I see what you have done now," said the King, " but I do not begrudge it. For I have never experienced the true wonder of music until this night, and I cannot live knowing that I will not experience such rapture again. Yet how can I betray the law of my fathers?"

"My Lord," said Celestine. "Is it not written that it is death for outsiders to willfully encroach upon the holy lands of this kingdom?"

"It is so written."

"Yet if I, royal born though of another land, were to sit upon the throne of this kingdom, I would not then be an outsider to this land?"

"You are wise," answered King Edric, and indeed his heart had grown full of love for Celestine. "If you will accept such as I, I would make you my Queen."

And so they were wed, for Celestine had also felt the stirrings of love within her heart for Edric, although not until the minute that she saw him weep for her music did she fully realize it. And Celestine's father, the old King, who had been grieving for a year for his lost daughter long thought dead, was informed by couriers from Edric's kingdom of her fate. So overjoyed was he to hear that Celestine was still alive that he immediately sued for peace with the people of Edric's kingdom, and proposed that their kingdoms be joined under the rule of Edric and Celestine. And so it came to be. The kingdoms were united and there was no longer fear of travel between the lands. The new Kingdom prospered, and there was trust where there once was fear, and there was music where once there was disharmony."

⪻ 14 ⪼

The following morning brought no new word from Vanaya and Garsen. After breakfast, Kinnemort announced that he was going to follow after them. Caroline could sense some apprehension in his expression, though he tried to disguise it. He left, admonishing Tegwyn to keep Caroline in sight at all times.

Caroline found that most of her strength had returned. Left to her own devices, she explored the interior of Vanaya's house. There was a mahogany bookcase in the main room with many dog-eared instructional books, catalogs and almanacs, dating from the late 19th and early 20th century, and printed in England or the United States. As she leafed through them, she noticed that several had pages torn out; others had parts marked out crudely with dark ink. One of the manuals, dealing with woodwork, had "Alabard" hand written on the inner cover in a delicate cursive script.

"Do you feel up for a stroll?" asked Tegwyn, distracting her from the books. "I can show you around the village."

"Sure. That would be nice."

"I hope you have enjoyed your time with us. I'll be sad to see you go."

"Oh, that's so sweet. I feel the same..."

"What is it, dear? The strangest expression just came over your face."

"I don't know. Nothing. I just suddenly got the sense that this house is very familiar somehow."

"Just *déjà vu*, I suppose," said Tegwyn. "The Good Mother taught us about that."

Tegwyn led Caroline outside. A frame terrace criss-crossed with vines extended several feet out from the front door. There was a hexagonally shaped rock garden planted with aster and butterfly weed just outside. Bearberry grew all along the fence surrounding the village.

The folk of Calendenny were out and about already, lugging pails of water, tending goats and pigs, or working in gardens and shops. One woman drove a horse-drawn wagon loaded with an assortment of vegetables. A group of men labored at fixing a jagged hole in the peat-covered roof of a nearby building.

"Terrible storm we had just last week," explained Tegwyn.

She led Caroline to a grassy commons in the center of the village. They sat cross-legged under a shady oak and watched the activity around them.

Caroline was suddenly struck by a thought.

"Tegwyn, are there other children here?"

"Children? No. I am the youngest in Calendenny. Why?"

"No children? It's just that...you know...don't you Elves, ummm...?"

"Don't we what?"

"Don't your people fall in love and get married?"

"Oh yes, of course we do. Vanaya and Garsen are bonded, as are many of the men and women of Calendenny. I believe that the Good Mother wedded Vanaya and Garsen herself. Now Vanaya blesses the bride and groom as Younger Mother of Calendenny."

"But there are no children?"

"No. Why? The Good Mother will bring more Elves into this world if she sees fit. And then one day she will return and take us all to the Other World. That is what Vanaya has taught us."

"Tegwyn, you know I'm not an Elf, right?"

"Of course, silly."

"How are you...how are Elves different from me?"

"Oh, you can't tell Elves from Humans just by looking, for the most part. It's our senses, our *faculties* that separate Elves from other peoples. It's our innate understanding of the world. Our ability to commune with the plants and animals and sense hurts in the earth as if it were a living thing itself."

"Do you remember the Other World?"

"No. The Good Mother told Vanaya that I was born in this world."

Caroline pondered Tegwyn's words and was silent for several minutes. She noticed a group of women heading down a dirt path branching off from the main village road and leading to a gap in the fence.

"What's that over there, where those women are going?"

"That's my special place," beamed Tegwyn. "It's very beautiful. Come and see!"

"Okay."

They left the breezy comfort of the shade and headed down the path. A man dressed in a worn leather smock stepped out of a shop they passed.

"Tegwyn," said the man, "Do not lead our visitor too far from the village. If the King's men come, we will need to hide her."

"Don't worry, Alabard. The King's men could not approach within a kilometer of Calendenny without us being aware of it. And besides, Caroline is with me. She couldn't be safer."

"Even so, have a care," replied Alabard with a laugh.

"Oh, so you're Alabard?" asked Caroline. "I saw your book on woodworking at Vanaya's house a while ago."

A puzzled expression crossed the man's face.

"I have no such book. I have always been the smith of Calendenny, as I have been instructed by the Good Mother's servants since my youth."

"Oh. I must be mistaken then."

"I'm only taking Caroline out to Anders Pond, Alabard. I will have her back inside before the sun rises over the top of the willows."

"Very well," Alabard said and retreated into his shop.

Tegwyn led Caroline down the path through the gap in the fence. Anders Pond, a picturesque saucer of still blue water, came into view. Willow trees lined the far side, but the near side was a gently sloping green glade, leading down to the pond. Ducks navigated the pond among water lilies, occasionally diving below the surface and bobbing up moments later.

"Isn't it nice?"

Tegwyn bent down and picked a purple aster.

"Wow. It's so beautiful. So peaceful."

There was a solitary outcropping of rock with one flat face centrally positioned in the glade.

"What's that? There's something drawn on it."

"Calen's Rock. Before a hunt we sing the hunting songs here. Andraya draws images of the quarry we seek on the flat face of the rock with colored chalk. It is Elven magic. Like our ability to commune with animals."

"You commune with animals?"

"Yes, we Elves have that gift."

Tegwyn stepped onto a small wooden fishing and diving pier jutting several feet out into the pond, sat down and languidly dangled her bare feet into the water.

"There's a beautiful swan that comes here sometimes, early in the mornings. I think she is one of the *Tylwyth Teg*. Vanaya told me that they sometimes take the form of animals."

"Have you ever seen one? I mean, aside from one in animal form?"

"No. You have to train yourself to see them, I think. One of these days I will have the mental discipline that I need to see the fair people."

"I see."

"They do love this pond, though. This is a known haunt of the *Tylwyth Teg*. It is said that if you leave a present for the good people and bathe in the waters of this pond afterwards, any hurt or illness you have will be healed. Oh, look at the ducks!"

A small platoon of them had waded out of the pond and fearlessly crowded onto the pier as their leader quacked out orders.

"Do you have some bread...?"

There was a sudden gust of wind, blowing Tegwyn's honey-hued curls in all directions.

"What the...?"

Tegwyn smiled mysteriously and turned away.

"Did she wear wild flowers in her hair?" she sang to herself.

Tegwyn's song was interrupted by the sound of a commotion and distant raised voices. A bell pealed in the distance.

Tegwyn jumped up.

"That is the alarm! Oh no, we must hide you!"

Caroline ran back up the pier, scattering the ducks, who dove out of her path and quacked in consternation.

"No, not that way! It sounds like they are in the village. Come this way."

She led Caroline along the side of the pond, into a thicket of brush.

"I know a path through here. If they are on horses, they will not be able to follow."

Caroline hurried after Tegwyn, feeling dry, brittle brush scrape across her arms. There was harsh shouting, now very close. She looked back and could faintly discern through the brush a man on horseback entering the glade. Tegwyn led Caroline to a sharp turn in the rapidly narrowing path. They reached a point where they were obliged to crawl through a narrow opening in a hedge. Caroline could now see that they had reached the far side of Anders Pond, beyond the row of willows. Ahead was a wide clearing and then another expanse of woods.

"Now we must run into the deep part of the forest. I think I can hide us there well enough, but we must cross this clearing first."

Caroline nodded, gasping for breath.

"Ready? Don't look back! Go!"

They sprinted through the thigh-high grass of the clearing. There was an unmistakable sound of galloping hoofs approaching from behind just as they reached the first outlying trees of the forested expanse before them.

"Oh, no!" cried Caroline. They were still too exposed and had obviously been sighted. The hoofs beat relentlessly closer. Then there was a thudding sound and the sound of a horse snorting. The hoof beats stopped.

Caroline looked back and saw the horse trotting in a confused manner, riderless. On the ground, someone struggled, arms pinned by a thick mesh. She turned back to Tegwyn and saw that the girl had stopped dead in her tracks. Four stocky figures were standing before them, blocking the path.

"Stop!" cried a voice, as Caroline began to turn to run the other way.

It was Tony. He stepped from behind a tree and ran up to Caroline.

"Tony! Oh thank God it's you!"

She embraced him warmly.

"Who are these people?"
"Dwarves!" spat Tegwyn.
"Dwarves?"
"Dwarves," said Tony.

$$\Leftrightarrow 15 \Leftrightarrow$$

Another stranger, this one with braided ginger hair, hopped out of the lower branches of a white ash behind Caroline, landing sprightly on his feet. He knotted the weighted net that snared the Wolf King's horseman as he cursed and struggled beneath it.

"There, there, chap," he chided the trapped man. "Do be a delight and keep still. Hello! What's this?"

He knelt down and picked up a matchbox-sized metallic object that had fallen beyond the reach of the net, handing it to Tony.

"It looks like a communications device, Rumil" said Tony, examining it from all angles.

"Like a radio?" asked the stranger standing in front of Caroline. He was a broad-shouldered man standing just over five foot three, with straw-colored hair and a short beard. He wore an earth-toned broad brimmed hat and a heavily patched jacket over an un-tucked shirt with greasy looking tails. His accent called to mind some remote backwoods expanse of Appalachia.

"Something like that. We can't stay here, Doren. We need to get back to the safe house. There's no telling if this guy has already sent word back to Selwys Castle, and we already know they're watching this village closely."

"And once they catch wind of what's happened here," said the one called Doren, "the Wolf King's men will be crawlin' all over this area. Come, girl," he said, nodding at Tegwyn.

Tegwyn stood rooted to the ground.

"Come!" he repeated in a more irritated tone of voice and took a step towards her.

Caroline stepped forward.

"Get away from her!" she warned, glaring at the man.

"Come on, guys!" broke in Tony. "We don't have time for this. We're all friends here. Tell your friend to come along, Caroline."

"We won't harm you, girl. We have our quarrels with the Elves, but we do not stoop to kidnapping. You will be returned when it is safe. Or perhaps you want to go back and take your chances with the Wolf King's men who will soon be occupyin' your happy little Elf village."

"Caroline, these guys are alright. They've been hiding me for the past couple of days and they helped me track you down. Your friend will be fine. Trust me."

Caroline relented. She took Tegwyn by the hand and they followed Tony and his new companions. Doren led them without hesitation through increasingly dense growths of forest, down winding animal paths, into dry gullies and ravines that appeared without warning under their feet and back up again. They continued for almost three hours without stopping, carefully stepping over puddles filled with musty leaves. Caroline thought she was about to collapse from exhaustion when Doren signaled everyone to stop. He whistled once and an echoing whistle came from a dense growth of Elderberry. Doren sighed and pushed aside some brush, revealing steps leading down to a pitted wooden door. They walked in.

Inside it was dark, the only light provided by the wobbly flame of a few tallow candles positioned about the room. Caroline made out three people sitting around a table in the center of the low-ceilinged room. Two stood up as soon as they entered.

"Vanaya! Garsen!" cried out Tegwyn, recognizing them immediately.

Vanaya embraced the girl, then turned to Doren with anger in her eyes.

"Why did you bring this one here?"

"It seemed a prudent course of action at the time, ma'am."

"The Wolf King's men surprised us when we were out by Anders Pond," explained Caroline. "Tegwyn led me away, but one of them caught up to us. That's when these guys showed up."

"And you are quite sure you were not followed, Doren?" demanded Vanaya.

"Oh, I shouldn't worry 'bout that. Even if the Wolf King's hirelings had the faintest idea in which direction we went, they could wander within sniffin' distance of our front door and never so much as suspect we were here."

"That was brave of you to help Caroline," said Vanaya, putting her hands on Tegwyn's shoulders.

"Vanaya, why are you here? Are we prisoners now?"

"We have come under a flag of truce. Garsen and I tracked Caroline's friend Tony to the Dwarf settlement of Kevello. We pled for audience with Doren so that we might discuss the situation posed by the Other Worlders. It was mutually agreed to move Tony to this safe house. We were planning to accompany a party of Doren's men to Calendenny to see about bringing Caroline here, but it seems Doren slipped out early this morning when we were resting. If he had not returned when he did, we would have swiftly been off on his trail."

The rest of the Dwarf men stationed themselves around the table, except for Rumil, who went back outside to stand guard.

"That was my fault, uh, Vanaya, was it?" said Tony. "When I heard that Caroline was at Calendenny, I convinced Doren and Rumil that we needed to get her out of there immediately."

"I'd say it worked out as best as it could've," said Doren. "Spies from Selwys surrounded Calendenny. If you had returned there and tried to sneak her out, you would have been snared for certain."

Tony could sense Vanaya bristling at Doren's suggestion, but she offered no retort.

"Fortunately the girl was already outside and fled right into our waiting arms, as it were."

"Sit down, Caroline," said Vanaya. "How is your leg feeling?"

"Not bad," Caroline answered, finding an unoccupied chair in a corner of the room. "I really think it's okay now. I'm tired from all the running and hiking, though."

She stretched her legs.

"So you guys are Dwarves, huh? Has anyone ever told you you're pretty tall for Dwarves?"

"This is your Caroline, Tony?" said the Dwarf man who had been sitting at the table with Vanaya and Garsen. He had deep lines carved in his forehead and sported a full, grey beard.

"She is every bit as fair as you had led us to believe."

"I don't think I said that, Poppa Narvil."

"Wait. *Fair*, Tony?" asked Caroline. "You said I was *fair*?"

"No," said Tony, feeling himself blushing again. "That is…I didn't say you were ugly or anything…"

"Shut up, Tony."

"Okay."

"Well, now that the Other Worlders are safe, we must decide what we are to do."

"No doubt, Vanaya," replied Doren, "but first things first. I am famished. Where is that Mirta? Mirta!"

In response, a rear entrance nearly hidden in darkness opened, revealing a diminutive, stout woman wearing a woolen shawl. Beyond the door was an open-air porch. A campfire had been built on the ground. Caroline could discern a familiar scent of frying meat.

"All right, I heard you the first time," replied the woman in a surly tone.

Two of the other Dwarf men went out to the porch and returned with plates of rectangular slices of meat. These were served with hard, thin bread sticks.

"Spam?" asked Caroline.

Doren cleared his throat and held up a mug.

"To your health, ladies and gentlemen. *Živjeli*."

Tony tasted the meat tentatively. It was flavored with some unfamiliar spices.

"There's somethin' mean in there," commented Doren.

"I'll hear no complaints from you," warned Mirta.

"Who's complainin'? It's parsable."

"*Parsable*. Hah! Will you listen to this man?"

"Oh, give me peace, woman, while I have my meal. Holy snapping duck…"

"Mind your tongue in front of the guests!"

"Where did you get this meat, Doren?" asked Tony.

"Shaw here procured a crate of it from one of the King's hirelings. It seems the Wolf King frowns upon this particular delicacy. The hirelings could not very well complain to a higher authority when they were relieved of a crate, or two, of it from their secret stores."

"You stole this from the Wolf King's men?" asked Vanaya incredulously.

"I would not make a big noise about stealing, thieving Elf jackdaws!" cried Mirta.

"Thieving? Are you making an accusation?" Vanaya stood up, anger flushing her face.

"My favorite mare was stolen from her stable in Kevello," said the man called Shaw. "Other beasts have disappeared."

"We have taken nothing from your people," replied Garsen in an even tone. "Yet Dwarf men were seen setting fire to fields we plant in common with the King's men, just two months past."

"By Korac's beard, have you ever heard such slander, Doren?"

"What proof have you?" demanded Doren.

"Cynthea saw two men in Dwarf garb fleeing the fields as they burned. And our harvest of peaches vanished last month. The trees were stripped bare of fruit in the night. Now we have taken to stationing sentries in our fields at all hours."

"Well that's just ridiculous," protested Doren. "Why would we be stealing fruit from Elves or settin' their fields afire?"

"Peaches?" asked Tony.

"Yes. Why, Tony?" asked Vanaya.

"Funny, but there was a storehouse packed to the rafters with peaches at Selwys Castle. I saw it when they had me hauling in bags of potatoes from the fields. I carried a bag inside and saw baskets and crates of peaches stacked everywhere, going bad by the smell of it. One of the Wolf King's men told me I was in the wrong storehouse and practically shoved me out."

"Hmm," said Caroline.

The Elves and Dwarves eyed each other with distrust across the table.

"What did your mare look like, Shaw?" asked Caroline.

"Amada. She was brown, with a white "mask" over her eyes."

"Did Amada do this little dance where she sort of trots in place and bobs her head when you bring food to her?"

"You have seen her? At the Elf village?"

"No. At Selwys Castle."

"Could she have just wandered away?" asked Tony.

"No. She would have returned. I am sure of it."

Caroline looked at Tony.

"Could the Wolf King be behind this whole feud?"

"Elves and Dwarves have ever been enemies," said Mirta obstinately.

"But why?"

"That's what we were taught from the time we came to this world," explained Shaw.

"As were we," said Vanaya.

"That's it?" asked Caroline drily. "You've always been enemies?"

"Told by who?" asked Tony.

"Well…we'd hear stories from…"

"From the Wolf King's flunkies?"

The Elves and Dwarves were silent. Vanaya looked flustered.

"What would the Wolf King gain by putting you at each other's throats?" mused Tony.

"I'm sure I don't know. He has ever been an enigma to us, as many aspects of life in this world are," conceded Vanaya.

"Speaking of that," interjected Tony, "now that Caroline's safe, all we need is to get beyond the borders of the Wolf King's territory, and we'll be gone. Out of your hair for good."

"Gone?"

"Yes. It's hard to explain, but the power that drew us here will fade and we will return to our own…world."

"But you cannot go beyond the borders of this land," said Poppa Narvil.

"Can't?" Tony looked around at all the faces around the table.

"Why can't we?" asked Caroline.

"It is death," Garsen said. "Everyone knows that."

"What do you mean? The penalty is death? We're probably facing that already."

"No," said Vanaya. "You would die. Some evil sorcery of the Wolf King would literally tear you apart."

"Wait," interrupted Caroline. "This is something you've actually seen? Or is this something you've been *taught*?"

"It is true," said Shaw. "My brother Padraeg, rest his soul, witnessed it. There was a man, like you an escapee from Selwys Castle.

He was picked up and flung about as by a great invisible creature. My brother would not have lied about such a thing."

"On no, Tony," said Caroline, sounding panicked for the first time. "You mean we're stuck here? Forever?"

"No. Not forever. We'll find some way out of here."

"But how?"

"The Wolf King. He has to have his own time ship, shuttle, whatever. We have to get back to Selwys Castle and find some way to take it."

"Could we sneak in?"

"It would be foolish to try," said Garsen.

"I doubt if we could figure out how to operate his equipment. We're going to have to capture him and *make* him return us to our time."

"But how, Tony?"

"Help us," said Tony, turning to Vanaya, and then to Doren. "I've only met this Wolf King once, but I'm sure he's behind everything, the burnt and stolen crops, stolen livestock. And worse, probably. You're living in fear of him, aren't you?"

"I'd call that a fair statement," allowed Doren, and Vanaya nodded in agreement.

"He's got what? Thirty men at most at Selwys Castle? Between the Elf and Dwarf communities, we have twice that, easily."

"It is impossible," said Vanaya tersely. "The Wolf King has powerful weapons. Weapons that will down a grown man at twenty meters. We would not even reach the gate if we stormed it openly. And that's not all. The Wolf King has creatures at his disposal. Things too terrifying to even speak of."

"I think you need to listen to Vanaya here," said Doren. "We daren't openly challenge the Wolf King."

Silence fell. The candlelight danced and cast odd, elongated shadows on the walls.

"Is there nothing you can do for Tony and Caroline, then?" pleaded Tegwyn.

"I...don't think..." began Vanaya.

"What about the Black Witch?" asked Tegwyn.

"The who?" asked Caroline.

"The Black Witch. She is a powerful sorceress who lives in the northwest part of this kingdom."

Everyone in the room turned to look at Vanaya.

"We know very little about her," Vanaya explained, "except that she dislikes company."

"But she is good!" Tegwyn protested.

"How do you reckon this, child?" asked Doren.

"She saved Garsen's life once."

"It is true," said Garsen. I suffered a terrible fall when hunting, three years past."

"We stood around Garsen," continued Vanaya, "quite sure that he was not long for this world. We could not even move him, because of the pain it caused. Suddenly, the Black Witch appeared. She told us that she would heal him, but we would have to depart. With heavy hearts we left him in her care."

"I remember being borne away to her dwelling somehow," said Garsen. "Beyond that, I have no memory. I woke weeks later alone in the woods, not far from Calendenny, fully healed."

"But what is her connection to the Wolf King?"

"None that we know of, Caroline," answered Vanaya. "She dwells in a remote corner of his kingdom. The Wolf King's men avoid her territory. It is said that the Wolf King himself fears her. She discourages all who intrude."

"Well, that doesn't sound very hopeful," said Caroline glumly.

"And yet," said Tony, "She did save Garsen's life. And she doesn't seem to too cozy with the Wolf King. Maybe she would help us."

"Black Witch? Like a black magician? Sounds like someone we should avoid."

"You misunderstand, Caroline," explained Vanaya. "She is dark skinned, as few in this land are. Darker than even you are."

"How do we find her?" asked Tony.

⟪ 16 ⟫

Vendela had been practically alone for almost two months now. The last remaining hired *husman* who farmed his own small tract of the *gard* had left a fortnight ago, seeking his fortune oversees and consigning Vendela to the mercy of the Almighty. Vendela had pleaded with him to stay, but refused the invitation to go with him. She was not yet ready to leave everything she had ever known behind based upon some vague rumors of a better life in a new land. And besides, she did not really trust the *husman*. He was a surly fellow at best and quick to anger. She had been the subject of his wrath more than once. When he realized that Vendela would not follow him, he finally threw his hands up, simultaneously cursed her stubbornness and muttered a benediction on her behalf and disappeared into the snow.

Vendela's faith in the imminent return of her father was unshakeable, at least until the time the *husman* left and she was truly alone. Every day she performed the same chores about the house and *gard* as if nothing had changed. But it was clear that food, firewood, and time were running out. A woman from a neighboring *gard* had been visiting from time to time to check in on Vendela and drop off some small provisions of cod or bread, but her visits were becoming increasingly infrequent as the winter wore on. On one occasion a snare Vendela had set had caught a hare. She skinned it and prepared it as she had seen her mother do years ago while she yet walked the earth. The stringy meat sustained her for days.

To take her mind off the hunger, she would pore through the journals of her father, Finne. She preferred to read the earlier ones, recounting his experiences in the war with the Swedes, who now claimed lordship over the entire country. But her favorite part was reading about how Finne had met her mother Grete, their brief courtship and eventual marriage. His later writings, following the death of her mother, were increasingly odd, confessional and agitated. He wrote about mysterious powers at work, and some sort of shadow government few people discerned, more powerful than the Swedes or even the Russians. It was difficult for her to understand, even though her reading level was very advanced for her tender years.

Vendela's father had spoken of days past before the war when the *gard* was prosperous and many *husmen* worked there, but every year there were fewer crops, fewer animals, and fewer *husmen*. He had proudly refused offers to sell the land. War and lean times came. Infertile fields lay fallow. The offers to purchase dried up with the crops.

Finne had finally left early one chill morning, promising a swift return. He would trek to a large neighboring *kommune* and offer what he still had of value from the days of the war in exchange for provisions that would sustain them through the remainder of the winter. That was in December, and it was now early February. Winter's grip on the land would not be soon released.

Vendela had finally resolved to attempt the march to the *kommune* in search of her father. She was now thin and emaciated, and the cold felt like a literal weight seeking to crush her frail frame. She would reach the *kommune* or die trying. Then the stranger arrived. He spoke with an accent. He asked Vendela why she was alone. He seemed shocked when she related to him how long she had been living alone.

"Can you take me to the *kommune*?" she asked him.

"Certainly. If that is where you want to go."

"My father must be dead."

"I fear that is the case."

"Sometimes I wish I had gone with the *husman* to the new land."

"My dear, I can take you to a new world."

"You can?"

"Yes. But you must assure me that is where you want to go."

Vendela pondered for a moment, looking around the *gard*. Idle farming implements lay frozen to the ground and long icicles, like the beards of giants of legend, hung from the main cottage and abandoned animal pens. Every detail she focused on called to mind memories of her life there – a sprained ankle from the time she tried to leap off the roof of a barn, a fright from a wayward bear that had strayed onto the *gard*, a boisterous wedding party for some relatives of the *husman*, a random memory of her mother laughing -- now all blurred and frozen together.

"I want to go," she said.

༺☙◉☙༻

Early the next morning, Tony, Caroline, Rumil and Garsen set out from the safe house. It was still almost two hours before sunrise. Mist clung to the ground in ephemeral pools and swirled around trees. They paused for a minute, taking stock of the provisions and equipment they carried.

"Are you sure you want to do this, Caroline?" asked Tony. He still felt half asleep, and uncombed patches of hair protruded at awkward angles from his head.

"Yes. No question. I miss my porch. I miss the nachos at Arnulfo's Family Restaurant. I miss my phone. I miss my Doc Martens. But most of all, I miss real bathrooms. As God is my witness, I will never use a privy again!"

"Okay, then! Lead on, Garsen."

"We will bear in a northwestern direction for about an hour until we reach the northern limit of the Verden Woods. From there the land becomes increasingly clear of trees and brush. We will have to hazard crossing some outlying crop fields of the Wolf King. Sometimes there are men, but they tend to avoid the place for fear of the Black Witch, we believe. We should be able to pass through unnoticed. Beyond that, we will be in the territory I only vaguely recall from my previous encounter with the Witch. May the Good Mother guide our steps and watch over us."

"I feel like Dorothy in *The Wizard of Oz*," quipped Caroline.

"Ha," grumbled Tony, mirthlessly.

"I know this story you speak of," said Garsen.

113

"You do?"

"The Good Mother read it to me when I was a child. May the Witch find your home for you, Caroline. And for you Tony."

"But will I find my courage?" asked Tony.

Rumil and Garsen bickered over the best course through Verden Woods, and they were slowed by a rain-swollen tributary to the Meddywyn, so they did not make as good time as they had hoped. The earliest rays of the morning sun were already filtering through the thinning forest canopy when they spied the wooden fencing marking the perimeter of the King's fields in the distance.

"Looks like a corn field," observed Rumil. "We should be able to walk through those stalks unnoticed."

Garsen said nothing, but Tony noticed a look of concern cross his face.

"I need a short break," said Caroline.

"Let's rest here then, before we're out in the no-man's land between the woods and the corn fields."

"Very well, Tony," agreed Garsen, scanning the landscape beyond the woods. Rumil produced a flask of Dwarf nog, which he passed around. Caroline found a clear spot in a patch of winterberry shrub and sat on the ground. She turned to Garsen.

"Yesterday Vanaya mentioned something about creatures the Wolf King keeps. We heard about a dragon when we were at Selwys Castle. Is that real?"

"I have never seen it," replied Garsen. "But I too have heard stories of this creature. I shudder to think of such a terror loosed upon my people."

"I have heard rumors of giant ogres," said Rumil. "A man at Kevello swears he spied two such monstrous creatures once, this past mid-Summer in the guarded regions away beyond Selwys Castle. Bigger than houses they were."

"Ogres? Elves, Dwarves, Fairies, Witches, and now Ogres? What next, Tony? Vampires? Zombies?"

"Oh, I sure hope not."

Something caught Caroline's attention.

"What is that?"

Caroline pointed to an odd bush growing on the edge of the clearing. It stood about three feet high, with six curved branches protruding like tentacles from the top of its stubby trunk.

"Yeah, what is that?"

Rumil walked over to it.

"This is a strange thing. I have never seen such a plant in any garden or forest in these lands."

They all gathered around it. Caroline gasped.

"I saw it move!"

"It is moving," agreed Garsen, incredulously.

"*Prokleti*! It is *breathing*, by Korac's beard!"

"You're right, Rumil."

"This is creepy," said Caroline. "I want to get out of here."

"I heartily concur," said Rumil. "Let us move on."

With a new sense of urgency, they cleared the edge of the woods and jogged through tall wild grass towards the King's fields. They reached the fence, breathing heavily from the exertion. Garsen gave Tony and Caroline a hand in climbing over.

"Stay close," cautioned Garsen.

Rumil pulled a short sword out of its scabbard.

"In case we should encounter one of the King's men," he explained.

"That is a sturdy looking blade," commented Garsen.

"I acquired it from one of the Wolf King's men," responded Rumil. "Well worth the trinkets I traded away for it."

"Some of my men have similar blades. Keep it handy."

The corn stalks dwarfed all of them, and there seemed little possibility that they could be spotted so long as they walked among them. Yet Tony felt an increasing claustrophobic sense of dread as they continued. The sun had fully risen by now. A chill morning wind blew through the field, shaking the stalks.

"It seems unnaturally quiet," mused Garsen. "There should be birds singing."

Caroline let out a surprised yell. They turned to her.

"What is it, Caroline?"

Caroline was looking around.

"Sorry. It was nothing I guess. It felt like something touched me on the shoulder, but I guess it was just the stalks blowing in the wind."

They paused briefly while Garsen studied the sun as it rose over the stalks. Rumil inspected the stalks growing nearest to him.

"These look like no corn stalks I have ever seen. Much too large, for one thing. Freakishly so."

There was another brief blast of wind, shaking the stalks back and forth.

"You know," said Tony, "I'm getting more and more of a weird vibe from this place."

"Shouldn't these things stop moving?" asked Caroline. "The wind has stopped now."

They traded glances. The stalks were swaying back and forth in an increasingly agitated manner.

"Gentlefolk, I suggest that a hasty strategic retreat from this area is called for. Now!" cried Rumil.

"Follow me!" urged Garsen. "Run!"

With an upward swing of his arm, Garsen used his bow to thrust back a stalk that suddenly blocked their path. Tony felt rough leaves like sandpaper brushing against his arms and legs as he fought his way through the stalks.

"Yah!" yelled Rumil, hacking at another intrusive stalk with his sword.

Out of the corner of his eye, Tony imagined he could see something emerging from the tops of the stalks. He blocked it out and concentrated on running as fast as possible while avoiding the grasping, leafy appendages that were now reaching into their path from both sides.

"Ugh!" screamed Caroline as they finally emerged from the stalks. The sleeves of Garsen's and Rumil's shirts were in tatters. They had borne the brunt of the assault, having led the charge. Tony felt a hot, raw burn where a leafy appendage had caught him across his left cheek and jaw. Caroline was mainly unscathed. They continued running even after they had jumped the fence at the far end of the field, finally collapsing on the ground when they located a shallow ravine that provided some cover.

"What were those things?" demanded Caroline.

"I thought I saw something," said Tony. "Something alive. I mean, not alive like plants, but like…I don't know. I thought I saw eyes."

"You did not imagine it," said Rumil. "Unless I experienced the same hallucination."

"What in the name of all that is good?" asked Garsen.

"I thought I saw…an arm," said Caroline.

Tony shuddered.

They decided to rest in the ravine and have a brief meal. Garsen passed out rations from a pouch he carried.

"We are getting close to the Witch's territory now. It's unlikely that we will be followed by the King's men at this point," he said.

"Well that's good to hear, I suppose," grumbled Rumil. "But these Elf rations leave much to be desired."

"It's not that bad," said Tony, chewing on some jerky.

"It is a travesty. A repast fit only for swine. A culinary nightmare. In summary: yuck!"

He threw the rest of his rations aside.

"Perhaps it would go down better with that swill you Dwarves call nog?" replied Garsen, raising an eyebrow.

Rumil looked stunned for a moment, then burst out with a laugh.

When they all had rested, Garsen surveyed the surrounding landscape and then led them out of the ravine. They passed into an area of gently rolling grassy hills. As they walked along, Tony noticed a long earthen wall snaking away to their left.

"Are there more fields of the Wolf King beyond that wall?"

"No," replied Garsen, "Or at least, we do not believe so. But we do not want to go that way."

"Why not?"

"It is an evil place. It would be death to go there. The Good Mother taught us this from the time we were children."

"As did Korac the Founder teach us Dwarves," said Rumil.

"You mean that's the border to the Kingdom? We would get ripped apart if we went there?"

"No, it is not the border. The Kingdom of the Wolf extends some distance beyond, it is believed," explained Garsen. "But that area beyond the fence we must also avoid."

Tony squinted but could see nothing beyond the wall but haze.

As they continued the march northward, they encountered another, larger river. Garsen led them over an unguarded footbridge. Beyond that, the land began to gradually slope downward. Caroline knelt down to pick something up.

"What is it, Caroline?" asked Tony, stepping to her side.

"It's a toy, I guess. It looks like horse. No, a deer. It has antlers, see?"

She held out a frayed woolen figurine, soiled and worn as if it had been lying on the ground, trodden over and exposed to the elements for years.

"One of yours?"

"It doesn't appear to be of Elf make," said Garsen.

Rumil shook his head.

"It makes me sad for some reason," said Caroline.

She set it down again and they continued wordlessly.

The grassy landscape gave way to more rocky terrain as they progressed. A path had been worn into the earth and they followed it. After another hour's march, a crumbling stone wall appeared ahead. The path led to a gap in the wall, the remains of a picket gate laying on the ground before it. A crow lit on the wall and crackled. Garsen, still in the lead, started to walk through.

They heard an inhuman croaking voice.

"You cannot go further!"

They halted in their tracks. The voice had come from the crow. Tony saw an expression of despair cross Caroline's face. He stepped forward.

"Um. Hello? My name is Tony Marco. This is my friend, Caroline Montano. We really could use some help. We were kidnapped by the Wolf King, you see..."

"You may continue, Tony and Caroline. You Elf, and you Dwarf, cannot."

❧ 17 ❧

Caroline and Tony said farewell to Rumil and Garsen after taking some small pouches of food and water from them. With reluctance, Tony also accepted a polished hunting knife from Garsen. Rumil offered his short sword to Caroline, but she refused it. They passed the gate and continued on the path. The terrain grew more level, and pine trees lined both sides of the trail, growing gradually taller as Tony and Caroline progressed. The trail disappeared into the distance with no apparent end in sight.

After another thirty minutes of hiking they took another break, having found a toppled red pine trunk on the side of the path to rest on. Tony and Caroline took the time to catch up on everything that had transpired since they split up after their flight from Selwys Castle.

"So you just bandaged yourself up out in the woods? That's crazy."

"It's just one of my many talents," said Caroline brightly. "Actually, it's something my Dad taught me. He was into this major survivalist thing. He taught us everything we needed to know if we were stranded alone out in the wild, or if the government collapsed or whatever. He had this fixation with water. Like every drop was precious. He would literally make us give prayers of thanks for water. We used to have to fill every empty bottle with water. We had a whole garage full of water bottles at one point, so there wasn't even room for anything else, much less the car. It was kind of crazy."

"I don't remember that."

"That was mainly after Elizabeth died. Before Mom and Dad got divorced."

"Oh, well you weren't coming around much then, so...sorry to bring that up."

"No, Tony!"

Anger flared in Caroline's eyes.

"It wasn't me who stopped coming around! It was you! I wanted you. I needed you. I needed my friend, and you ignored me. When you saw me at school you ran the other way!"

Tony sat, stunned. Was that really the way it had happened?

"I...I don't know what to say, Caroline. I'm sorry. I'm so sorry."

Caroline turned away, covering her face with her hands. She angrily blinked back tears.

"Oh, forget it." She jumped to her feet. "Come on. I can't wait any longer. The suspense is killing me. Let's go see this damn Witch."

The path wound westward for a short distance and then resumed in a northerly direction. The pines gave way to patches of colorful wildflowers stretching out on either side of the path.

Caroline sniffed the air. "Are we close to the shore?"

"Wait, I think I see something," said Tony. "Is that a chimney?"

Caroline and Tony stepped forward cautiously. They could now clearly see a white one-story wood frame house with a gabled roof at the end of the path. Full sized arched windows were set on either side of the front door, which had a decorative mat laid before it.

"That looks like a painting my Grandma had in her living room," said Caroline.

"Huh. Looks a bit too Norman Rockwell for the 11th Century."

"Maybe we're not really in the 11th Century."

"Could be, I guess," said Tony, doubtfully. "What's that?"

A low, pulsing sound was heard.

"It doesn't seem loud, but I can feel it shaking my ear drums, like when a helicopter flies by," said Caroline.

"Morse code, maybe? Maybe she's trying to tell us something?"

They continued to approach the house slowly. As they got closer they could see that the landscaping had obscured a water filled ditch surrounding the house. It was wide, more than thirty feet across. Tony walked up to the concrete embankment.

"Looks deep. And it smells like salt water."

"Can we swim it?"

A splashing sound made them both turn their heads. A gray triangular fin emerged from the water. Another one popped up beside it.

"You've got to be kidding me," said Caroline. "Are those sharks?"

"I'm not sure."

"What are we supposed to do? Is this some sort of game?"

The rhythmic pulsing abruptly stopped.

"Not a game, Caroline Montano," said a disembodied voice, similar to the one they had heard before, but louder. "It is a test."

"What kind of test?"

"The path is before you both," continued the voice, enigmatically.

They heard a whirring sound. From the concrete embankment extended a silvery plank. It stopped after it had extended several feet over the water.

"Tony," said the voice.

He looked at Caroline.

"I guess this is my ride."

Tony stepped onto it. It was clearly not metal despite the color. Some sort of synthetic polymer, Tony guessed.

A second plank extended from the concrete embankment some twenty feet apart from the first.

"Caroline."

Caroline stepped onto the second plank without hesitation.

"Wait," commanded the voice.

A T-shaped pole rose out of the water at about the halfway point of the ditch between the two planks.

"Proceed correctly, and the platforms will carry you to the far side. If you err, they will stop and begin to retract. However, if you should falter, you can still press the button at each end of crossbar of the center pole, provided that you can reach it, and the platform will safely carry you to the other side. But the button cannot be activated until you have made a mistake. And the button on your side will only work for the platform you are on."

"What does she mean, proceed correctly?" asked Caroline.

Tony examined the plank before him. It was covered in a pattern of squares, four rows total. Each square was big enough to stand in. As he observed, letters became visible on each square. The first row read A-B-X-R left to right. The next three rows were W-D-T-G, then Z-L-G-Y and finally F-M-N-C.

"Huh? There are letters on the squares."

"Numbers on mine," said Caroline.

"What is the pattern, Tony?" demanded the voice sternly.

"Pattern?"

"The design of creation. The pattern of life. The code. The weapon of your enemy."

"Weapon. Time? I'm supposed to spell something?"

There was no answer.

"Code of life," Tony mused to himself.

Something stirred in his memory.

"DNA? DNA? That has to be it! Okay. What was it? Base pairs of DNA?" he asked himself aloud. "Guanine, Thymine…Adenine!"

Tony stepped onto the square marked "A." It lit up as he stepped on it. The platform extended about a quarter of the way across the ditch.

He looked at the next row of letters, W-D-T-G.

"Adenine forms a base pair with…Thymine or Guanine? Which is it, T or G?" Tony searched his memory to no avail.

Tony shrugged and hopped onto the square that read "T." It lit up. The platform continued and stopped the halfway point, even with the t-pole in the middle of the ditch. On the third row he stepped onto the square that read "G" for Guanine. The platform moved to the three-quarter mark.

"Now what was the other DNA base?"

He paused and studied the final row of letters, F-M-N-C.

"What about me?" demanded Caroline, watching as Tony made his way across.

"What is the pattern, Caroline?" asked the voice.

Four rows of numbers appeared before her on the platform. The first, left to right read 4-9-3-7, then 8-1-9-5, 5-6-7-8 and 2- 8-9-6.

"I don't know anything about genetics."

"That is not your test. What was the sequence you heard?"

"What's she talking about Tony?" Caroline yelled.

Tony looked back.

"Sequence?" Tony concentrated for a moment. "Wait, remember that pulsing sound we heard? Was that a repeating sequence?"

"It was! The same thing over and over."

"Can you remember it? I don't think I can."

"I think so. I'm always unconsciously counting things, and we heard it so many times it's like it was branded on my brain. It definitely started with three pulses."

Caroline stepped onto the square marked with "3." It lit up and the platform extended to the one-quarter point across the ditch.

"Good going!" yelled Tony, turning back to watch Caroline's progress and forgetting his own predicament momentarily.

"The next one was five." She moved forward to the "5" square on the second row. Her platform continued to the halfway point.

Suddenly Tony remembered the final DNA base.

"Cytosine!" he said to himself, "It's Cytosine." But he still did not turn from watching Caroline's progress.

"What was the next one, Caroline?"

"Quiet!" she yelled. "I'm trying to concentrate. I need to hear it!"

"Sorry!"

Caroline closed her eyes in concentration. She played the sequence back in her memory. *Thrum Thrum Thrum, Thrum Thrum Thrum Thrum Thrum.*

"The final number was two. I'm sure of it. Three, five, then a long sequence, and then two. But was it seven or eight?"

"I know you can do it, Caroline."

"Eight. I think it was eight."

Caroline stepped onto the square marked "8." It did not light up. Caroline looked from side to side uncertainly. There was a humming sound. The platform began to tilt downwards to the ditch.

"No!" yelled Tony. "Go back, Caroline!"

Caroline turned around. There was a sudden jolt and the platform detached itself from the concrete embankment. With a tremendous splash it landed on the water, and floated in the middle of the ditch. The impact sent Caroline sprawling, but she quickly leapt to her feet again. The grey fins swam closer.

"The button must be pushed to save Caroline," said the voice.

"The button! Can you reach the button, Caroline?" Tony yelled.

"I don't know."

Caroline moved to the edge of the platform closest to the center pole.

"It's pretty far away. If I stretch I think I can reach it without falling in."

She could see a round, palm-sized yellow button at the end of the crossbar on her side. She swiped at it. Her fingertips brushed across the button, but the force of her desperate grab only caused the cross bar to swing around so that it was now pointing back towards the embankment.

"Hold on!" Tony said, running back to the mid point of his platform.

"Oh, Tony. I think I'm starting to sink!"

"Don't panic! I can reach it!"

"No you can't! You'll fall in! Go on without me, Tony."

"No, Caroline. I won't let you down." Under his breath he added, "Ever again."

Tony gauged the distance, took a deep breath, and leapt from the edge of his platform to the center pole. He grabbed the crossbar, swinging it back in the opposite direction with the momentum of his jump.

"Tony!"

He was hanging from the crossbar, with his right hand still about three feet away from the end. Tony tried sliding his hands sideways along the bar to get closer to the yellow button. He felt his hands slipping off the smooth surface of the crossbar. Gasping for breath, he made one final effort to get a firm grip with his left hand, then stretched his right arm as far as it would go and clapped his hand over the button. He felt the button depress just as his left hand lost its grip. Tony plunged into the water awkwardly and sank like an anchor, feeling no strength left in him after the effort.

For a second Tony felt and sensed nothing. Then his head broke the water and he coughed and gasped for air. He heard a high pitched chattering call and felt himself being gently propelled through the water by something warm and powerful beneath him. As he lost consciousness he imagined that he could understand the strange, alien voices and they were saying, *Come and live with us in our sunless, wondrous world beneath the waves, Tony. Come and stay with us forever.*

⋙ 18 ⋘

"**W**ho was the first ruler of a united Kingdom of England?" asked Mrs. Livingston.

"Huh? Where am I?" asked Tony. He tried to clear the fog from his head. He was sitting in an empty classroom in an antiquated school desk. Mrs. Livingston, wearing a Diaz Panthers t-shirt, stood with arms folded, leaning back against her desk at the front of the classroom.

"Pay attention, Tony. You are being tested."

"It was Athelstan. He was the first ruler of a united England, in the early years of the Tenth Century, A.D."

"Correct. In what year was the Christian *reconquista* of the Iberian Peninsula completed?"

"1492."

"When did the Austro-Hungarian Empire fall?"

"End of World War I. 1918."

"Who was the first woman in space?"

"The Soviet cosmonaut Valentina Tereshkova."

"Whose death prompted the Surgeon General of the United States to speak out against the "insidious incubus of internet addiction," and proclaim a national epidemic?"

"Um?"

"Oh, sorry. Getting ahead of you there. In what year did Christopher Columbus set off on his fourth voyage to the Americas?"

"1502."

"And was this a good thing?"

"What?"

"Was this voyage a good thing?"

"It was a historical event. It can't be quantified as good or bad. It is just something that occurred."

"Important events may be shaped by chance and natural factors — disease, famine, prosperity, even weather – but the thoughts and desires of men, whether those of the most pious men and women or those of the most shameless rogues are often the driving hand on the tiller of history. History isn't just names and dates, Tony. It is a vast and dense panoply of intersecting lives; a world changing force driven by dreamers, schemers, nobles and rascals, kings and peasants, saints and sinners, circumstances and random chance."

Caroline threw herself down on her bed. She could hear barking outside.

"Bosco! Leave that cat alone!"

She moved the palms of her hands back and forth across the smooth fabric of the comforter, luxuriating in its cushioned coziness.

"You look tired," said Elizabeth, standing at the door.

"Oh! You startled me," said Caroline, sitting up quickly. "It's been a while since you were here."

"I guess it has."

"We had planned to do so many things. Weren't you going to cut my hair? We have so much to catch up on."

"Yes, *chulita*. We'll have time for that now. How about that boy you once told me about?"

"Oh, him. That was nothing. And that was so long ago that I told you about him…"

Caroline paused in confusion.

"Is something wrong?"

"No. I'm fine. Only...can you answer a question?"

"What is that, *chulita*?"

"What's it like to be dead?"

"Who are you?" demanded Tony.

For a second, the classroom faded and he sensed he was in a dome-shaped chamber. Caroline was sitting nearby, eyes unfocused, opening and closing her mouth wordlessly. A clear disc on a metallic tentacle hovered over her head.

"What are you doing to Caroline?"

"I'm just talking to her. She's fine."

"Are you the Black Witch?"

The classroom reappeared around Tony. Caroline was there, sitting beside Tony. She groaned.

"What the…?"

Mrs. Livingston laughed.

"Is that what they call me? My real name is Paz. I am a scientist and a historian. Or I was. My area of study was data compilations in societies. Do you realize that, even with near-infinite storage space for data, nearly all data compilations, histories, and compendiums of knowledge of any sort are eventually forgotten or abandoned? It's a pattern that repeats throughout history. I know, not terribly interesting. Now, I am mainly an observer."

"Are you from the time of the Wolf King?"

"Wolfgang? No. He is a child of the first era of time travel, in the late 21st Century."

"Why are you both here then?"

"I was here before him. I was here watching when the Romans, iron heeled and arrogant, walked this land. Then centuries later, the warlike Norsemen made homes here until they were driven out. I was here when the people who had driven out the Vikings were in turn ousted by the arrival of the Wolf King, descending like an enraged Zeus from Mount Olympus. I watched as he and his followers gave fanciful, meaningless new names to the burned and vandalized settlements he rebuilt, and to the hills, the woods and the streams. And I have seen the displaced peoples return again and reclaim this land and finally complete the dismantling and destruction of "Selwys Castle," now associated with the supernatural terrors of their distant cultural memory, years after the fall of the Wolf King. But that has not yet occurred at this point in time."

"So the Wolf King just randomly came here to the exact same place after you did?"

"It is not that simple, Tony Marco. This is an important place in space/time. I might yet tell the full tale, or at least what I know of it, at some point. However, now is the time for you, and for you, Caroline, to answer my questions."

For a second it seemed to Tony and Caroline that it was no longer Mrs. Livingston standing in front of them, but a very old and small woman, seemingly of Afro-Caribbean descent with graying hair tied with bright red cords, and dark, piercing eyes.

"What do you want to know?"

"I want to know what you desire, Tony Marco."

"I – we -- both of us just want to go home."

"Quite. Quite. But there is a whole new life, a whole new set of possibilities open to you now. I think you want to see more."

"Yeah. Maybe. At some point, if I could control it."

"Control! Very interesting that you said that. Where would you go, if you could?"

"In time? I'd go back and see how the pyramids in Egypt and in the New World were built. I'd go back and see who were the first people in the New World. I'd go back and witness first hand the invention of agriculture, language, domestication of animals. I'd go back to see what the dinosaurs really looked like. What the earth looked like before life even existed on land."

"Such a thirst for knowledge you have! But are you mentally prepared to absorb such grand vistas, if opened to you? Could you so blithely witness the follies, the depredations, the iniquities, the ghastly horrors of history? Do you know how many people perished as a result of the Spanish Inquisition, or in the conquest of the New World by the Europeans? Could you casually witness the fate of the children Crusaders first-hand and not be scarred for life?"

She paced back and forth along the front of the classroom.

"Can you look into the eyes of men or other creatures who lived thousands or millions of years ago, knowing that they perished eons ago leaving not even the faintest trace either in dust or history, and yet recognizable thoughts, emotions, or even instincts lie there, linking you inexorably across the gulf of years? Can you withstand the howling void of Deep Time?"

She paused, raising a hand to her temple, as if she were in pain.

"As we sit here today, Tony, mighty civilizations rise and fall in the New World. Europe sits in darkness, still divided into squabbling petty kingdoms but striving for order, upset by migrations and beset by invaders. Yet in the Near and Far East, great advances in mathematics, science, technology and even literature have already been made which will have far-reaching implications for the next millennia and beyond. Are you familiar with Murasaki Shikibu, the Japanese noblewoman who penned *The Tale of Genji*, considered by many to be the first modern novel of world literature? Or Omar Khayyam? Mathematician, astronomer, poet, and philosopher, a true Renaissance man hundreds of years before Europe's reawakening. Can you imagine speaking to such a man? He walks the earth today."

"I've heard of him."

"But you have seen none of the momentous events of this era, in this little bubble of time, or "Temporal Proprietary" as the Wolf King would have it, along with these other foster children of time."

"It does sound a bit overwhelming. Scary."

"Ah, fear. That's it. You have always been the cautious one, haven't you? You fear unknown situations. Knowledge is what makes you safe. It is your power, your strength, your way to control situations. Your thirst for knowledge is driven by your desire for control."

"How would you know anything about me?"

"I have my ways of divining things. Your stars, the shape of your skull."

"Astrology? Phrenology? Those are pseudo-sciences, like Alchemy." She laughed.

"Ah, but my true methods would still seem as magic in your time. If one can travel through time, is it so strange to believe that one can *see* through time?"

"So you're going to foretell my future?" asked Tony, dubiously.

"No. You will have to meet your future and deal with it with no assistance from me."

"Hmm."

"Now something is troubling you."

"Well…"

"Go on."

"Mr. Gaudet was telling us that time isn't so much a linear thing as this big, interwoven…"

"Tapestry."

"Tapestry of moments. Like it all exists at once. And you can jump to one location in time to another like it's a big football field, but you can't rewind the clock. You can't alter anything, because wherever you are, you're part of the chain of events. You were *always* part of the chain. Tapestry."

"Yes."

"So, if you can't change anything, and the pattern is set, I'm basically just acting out a predetermined script. No choice I make matters, ultimately."

"Tony. What you do matters. Your actions are not predetermined. When you are confronted by momentous decisions, you will act guided by your intellect and by your conscience. And what arises of your own free will and the consequences thereof will be woven into history."

"What about me?" asked Caroline.

"I know what you desire, Caroline. Alas, it is beyond my power to give you. Like Tony, you will have to march out and greet your future as best as you can, guided by your head and your heart. Do not be overly troubled. You and Tony still have much to do. The test does not end here. You must prepare yourself for your greatest challenge yet."

Caroline looked crestfallen. Tony looked at Caroline questioningly and then back at Paz.

"Well, Tony, it seems that on this little adventure you have found your courage, and perhaps your heart. Now you both must use that marvelous brain of yours to find your home."

"Can't you just send us back?"

"I'm afraid you will have to face the Wolf King."

"Will you help us then?"

"I cannot fight your battles for you."

"Are you going to turn us into superheroes, then? Make us super strong or give us rays that shoot from our eyes?" asked Caroline.

Paz chuckled.

"You kids don't realize it, but you are already practically superheroes to us old folks. So young, strong, and fearless, unbent by the toil of years and not jaded by the workings of the world. You are the envy of us all."

"I still don't feel very fearless," said Tony, doubtfully.

"You two have just about everything that you need to defeat the Wolf King within yourselves. But I will give to you one thing that will help: a device that will nullify his long-range energy weapons. It is not a weapon, nor a shield. It will get you inside Selwys Castle with some help. A small army will do. Solve the riddle of Kevello and Calendenny and you will have your army."

"Riddle?"

"The rest is up to you. Farewell."

❧ 19 ❧

Tony opened his eyes and found himself looking straight up into a clear late afternoon sky streaked by wispy cirrus clouds. He sat up. Caroline stirred beside him.

"Where are we?" she asked groggily.

"Looks like we're back on the trail to the Witch's — to Paz' — house. Except that I can't see the house anymore. We must be some distance away from it now."

Caroline sprang to her feet.

"Look!" she said. Sitting on a patch of grass beside the trail was an obsidian five-sided obelisk, about a foot high, mounted on a varnished wooden base.

"A gift from Paz?" asked Tony.

Tony picked it up. A faint red light rhythmically pulsed from its center, diffusing through the dark, glassy exterior. Tony stared into it. There seemed to be an entire universe within the obelisk, liquid and shifting, vast and intimidating.

"Like a nebula..." he said out loud.

"Tony."

Where was he?

"Tony!"

Caroline's voice called him back to the present.

"I feel as if I've forgotten something."

"The Wolf King? Storming the castle?"

Tony set the obelisk down gently.

"Never mind this now. We need to figure out what it is that Paz wants us to do."

Tony sat down cross-legged in the grass and Caroline sat facing him, the obelisk between them.

"Paz told us to solve the riddle of Kevello and Calendenny. What did she mean, Tony?"

"I think I have an idea. But wait, what was that other thing she said? Something about not being able to help you?"

Caroline looked down again.

"Caroline, what is it? Can I help?"

Caroline stared into the ground for a while as if concentrating, then looked back up at Tony.

"Remember when Elizabeth died? It seemed as if there was no warning. But actually she had developed this mysterious nerve condition a year before that. Something that caused uncontrollable trembling, in the arms and legs, like Parkinson's disease. The doctors were completely baffled."

Caroline closed her eyes.

"Six months ago I started having the same symptoms."

"Oh Caroline. No. It can't be true. Have you seen doctors?"

"Yes. They still don't know anything. They're not even sure if it is directly related to my sister's death at this point. She had other latent health issues. So maybe it's nothing serious. My symptoms aren't too bad so far."

They sat quietly for a minute. Tony felt as if the ground had suddenly vanished from beneath him and he was floundering in mid-air, looking for a toehold on solid earth again.

"Have you ever been in love, Tony?"

The question caught Tony off guard.

"Well, I..."

He trailed off and looked away, pretending that there was something suddenly very interesting about the fields of wildflowers nearby.

Caroline laughed.

"Yeah. You don't really know, do you? I don't know either. You know, I was "going out" with a guy for several months last semester."

"What? Who?"

"His name is Raymond. I don't know if you know him."

"That guy who was always wearing the same school jacket all winter? Randomly throws boxer punches around when he's walking down the hall?"

"Yeah. That guy."

"Seriously? So what happened?"

Caroline chuckled. Tony sensed that she had discerned his distaste and reddened in embarrassment.

"Nothing, really. When we were together, I told him that I liked him and I cared for him. I actually told him that I loved him. I would say those words, but it was like I was just doing what I thought I was *supposed* to be doing and saying. Like when I was a little girl and I would play dress up with my Mom's clothes, except now I'm playing dress up with adult emotions that I don't even understand. And will I even live long enough to understand them now?"

"I'm so sorry I wasn't there for you."

"Tell me, Tony. Was there ever a girl that you felt something really special for?"

"Well. This is going to sound goofy, but…"

"Yeah? Go ahead."

"One time around two years ago, I went with my Dad on a business trip to Del Rio. We stopped in a hole-in-the-wall restaurant in a town called Uvalde along the way. There was this girl about my age there, sitting with her folks at one of the tables. She looked and me and our eyes just locked."

Caroline laughed. Tony flushed again.

"Oh, I'm sorry, Tony. Go on with your story."

"There's nothing more to say. I saw her just that once. We never even spoke."

"But you *knew*. Just like when you meet some people you instinctively know that you can be the greatest friends, hang out and talk about the most personal things. And then there are others where you immediately know that you have absolutely nothing in common, and they would never have anything remotely interesting to say in a hundred years. That's the way I feel with most of the girls my age."

"Yeah, I guess."

"I like that story. But you're going to have to learn to talk to girls. You probably shouldn't lead off with *I think you have a cute butt* next time."

"Oh my God."

"Hey, you're okay, Tony."

Caroline patted him on the shoulder.

I'm so sorry I got you into all this."

"Hey! It was me who pushed you into it. I'm just dumb sometimes, I guess."

"I meant this whole escape attempt. It's been a complete fiasco."

"We had to try."

"I guess. But maybe if we had stayed we could have figured out some other way. Some way to sneak into the castle. I don't know. Maybe the whole thing is futile. Feudal."

"What?" asked Caroline with a giggle.

"Nothing."

"I got that. You know, you're really funny and clever sometimes, Tony."

"Just sometimes?"

"Ha. But it's like you try to disguise it when you're hanging out with Carson and that crowd. Like you just want to be one of the *dudes*. You shouldn't do that."

Tony shifted uncomfortably on the ground.

"Remember that time we were in your room and you were singing that Christmas song from the school play? That *voice* you sang in. I nearly peed myself laughing."

Tony laughed in spite of himself at the memory.

"Anyway, don't beat yourself up about the whole escape thing. We had to get out of there. I wouldn't have wanted to stay another day. I didn't tell you this before, but remember that guard Gerard?"

"Yeah. I *hated* that guy."

"Me too. But there was this one time when I was sorting strawberries in one of the storehouses and suddenly he started talking to me. You know...*talking*. Like he wanted to know me."

"Ugh."

"Yeah. And then another guard came up to him and told him that the Wolf King wanted to speak to him. Later that day I saw Gerard and he looked like a whipped dog. He never said another word to me."

"That's kind of creepy."

"Yeah."

"You know, I wasn't even considering that before. I mean, it wasn't exactly a concentration camp, but if one of the guards or the Wolf King had gone psycho on you or me, what could we have done? God, I have tunnel vision, sometimes."

"That's okay, Tony."

There was a rustling in the brush nearby and they both jumped to their feet. A brown hare furtively emerged, disapprovingly twitched its nose in their direction and then hopped across the path. They laughed in relief.

"Too bad Paz didn't give us super powers," sighed Caroline.

"I have super powers."

"Oh, really?"

"Yes. I am invincible at mini-golf. Come on, what's your super power? You must have one."

"Um, I can play a drum roll by holding drumsticks between my toes."

"I had no idea you were so musically inclined."

"Aw, that's nothing. My real super power is being able to instantaneously read a page of internet posts and type snarky responses as appropriate. Faster than the conscious mind can process."

"Impressive."

"It comes in handy. And I'm challenging you to a game of mini-golf when we get back to Corpus, wise guy."

"I'll try to take it easy on you."

Caroline sighed.

"Ah, this is fun, like the way we used to talk."

Tony nodded.

"Now you have to tell me what your kryptonite is, Tony."

"Wires for me. When they get all tangled up. I hate that."

Caroline laughed. "Mine is women with painted-on eyebrows. I get this creepy feeling that they're really robots underneath."

"Do you feel like walking, Caroline? I kind of want to get out of here anyway."

"Sounds good to me."

Caroline picked up the obelisk. They got back on the trail and headed in the direction of the stone gate. A more solemn mood settled over them as the sun began to set.

"So what was that you said you'd figured out?"

"Well obviously," said Tony, "The people at Kevello aren't really Dwarves. And the folks at Calendenny aren't Elves."

"Well, duh. Did you tell them?"

"No, I didn't mention anything about it. I felt it would be raining on their parade. They seemed so proud of being Dwarves."

"Yeah, I know. It was the same story with the Elves. They had their own customs and songs and stories and everything. But that can't be the solution to the riddle, can it? It's too obvious."

"It's also pretty obvious that the Wolf King is behind it. The Dwarves kept talking about this man named Korac the Founder. Someone who taught them everything about Dwarf life and customs from the time they were children. He basically indoctrinated them to believe they were actually Dwarves."

"Again, same with the Elves, except it was a woman. The Good Mother. What was the name? Endewyn? I wonder who she was, really? Not that creepy Neon Sparrow girl, I hope. They almost worshipped her. It would be really sad, but there's something oddly romantic about it. There's something about Calendenny. It's like when you're there you can believe that there really is magic, and little invisible fairies in the garden."

"Hmm."

"Anyway, back to the riddle."

"Okay. It's also clear that the Wolf King was plotting to set the Elves and Dwarves against each other. They were conditioned to distrust each other from the time they arrived. Remember Rumil and Garsen talking about knives? The Wolf King was arming both sides."

"That's sick," said Caroline, shaking her head. "And he's been doing this for a long time."

"Yes, if he kidnapped these people when they were children. Poppa Narvil and Vanaya are both what? Around fifty years old?

"Probably not even that old. They just aged prematurely. But do you remember that Court Reporter thing?"

"Yeah."

"It mentioned dates that were over sixty years apart."

"The Wolf King can't be that old. Remember, Gaudet told us that people of the Wolf King's time don't have significantly greater life spans than people in our time."

"Yeah, but he's a time traveler. He could have arrived here around seventy years ago and set up shop, then had his goons kidnap the people who would become the Dwarves and Elves, zipped back to his time, and then returned thirty or so years later when they were adults."

"That still leaves up to forty years unaccounted for."

They continued down the path, quiet and pensive. The sun reddened as it sank into the western horizon.

"By the way, were there Dwarf children?"

"No, come to think of it. I noticed but I didn't ask about it."

"Tegwyn told me that there were no children in Calendenny besides herself."

"The Wolf King must have done something to them when he kidnapped them. But why wouldn't he want them to have children? To control their numbers, maybe? So they wouldn't turn against him?"

They could now see the stone fence that marked the outer borders of the Black Witch's territory in the distance.

"But there's still more to this," said Tony. "I noticed some odd things when I was at Kevello."

"Such as?"

"Like..."

Tony paused, concentrating.

"Like Kevello was old. Older than all the Dwarves. Even older than Poppa Narvil. I don't think they built it in the first place. There were some newer buildings, and some that looked like they had been rebuilt, but the workmanship wasn't nearly as good as on the older structures."

"Rebuilt. That reminds me of something."

"Did you get a sense that the Elves you stayed with built Calendenny?"

"No. In fact they admitted that Calendenny had always been there, from the time they arrived."

"Could Kevello and Calendenny just have been normal human villages that were abandoned when the Wolf King came here? Paz mentioned something about him driving out the native people."

"I guess it's possible."

Caroline shrugged.

"Think. What else do you remember?"

"Oh! When I was eating with them I saw a mug that had Vanaya's name on it and her picture. Except the picture had the wrong hair color, brunette instead of blonde. And then there was a book on wood-working with Alabard's name on it, but he denied it was his."

"Curious."

They reached the stone wall and passed through the gate, continuing on the path.

"Also, I noticed something freaky about Tegwyn."

"What's that?"

"When we were out by Anders Pond the wind was blowing her hair, and I could have sworn I saw pointed ears on her."

"I was starting to wonder if I had imagined that myself. Her hair was nearly always covering her ears."

"Wait! I just remembered something else. When I was at Vanaya's house I couldn't put my finger on it, but something was giving me a sense of déjà vu."

"What was it?"

"I realize now that the house was reminding me of the servants' quarters at Selwys Castle."

"How so?"

"It looked like it had been rebuilt. After a fire."

They heard a long whistle, followed by two short whistles.

"That's the signal from Rumil. I'll give him the all clear sign."

Tony crossed his arms in front of him twice. Rumil and Garsen popped out of a shallow ditch at the side of the path.

"Thank the Good Mother you are safe, Tony and Caroline," said Garsen, sounding genuinely relieved.

"About time you got here. This Elf was such a joy to keep company," grumbled Rumil, sardonically.

"If I had been forced to endure even one more Elf joke..." Garsen said, trailing off.

"Garsen. Rumil. I need to see something," said Tony.

The sun had fully set by the time they reached the earthen wall, and a blustery, chill wind blew over the somber landscape.

"I beg you to reconsider, Tony," Garsen pled.

"I have a hunch we'll find the answer to all the riddles here."

Before anyone could stop him, Tony found a foothold in the side of the wall and climbed over. The others paused, looking at each other.

"Come on, guys" said Tony from the other side of the wall. "I'm fine. There's nothing to worry about."

Caroline clambered over the wall, followed by Rumil and Garsen.

The grass was long on the other side, and it swayed in the wind.

"Those look like..." began Garsen.

"Markers," finished Rumil.

Tony walked up to a mound of rocks and earth. There were similar mounds scattered around in the area enclosed by the earthen wall.

"This one has something scratched on it. I can't make it out," said Caroline, studying one of the rock mounds.

"This one over here has flowers someone laid. Not that long ago," observed Rumil, examining another.

"It cannot be!" gasped Garsen in surprise.

They turned to him. He was kneeling in front of a mound with a squared stone laid on one end. Marked with chalk on the stone was the name "Vanaya."

The sun had not quite risen by the time they reached the safe house the next day. Tony, Caroline, Vanaya, Garsen, Tegwyn, Rumil, Doren, Mirta, Shaw, and Poppa Narvil solemnly stood around the table. Tony wasn't sure whether it was the shadows or the sense of occasion, but it suddenly seemed that he was in a room full of titans.

"So there is no doubt in your minds then?" asked Vananya.

"None," replied Tony. "There was another Calendenny, and an-other Kevello."

He turned to each member of the assemblage in turn.

"You are not Elves and Dwarves. You are all normal, mortal men and women like Caroline and me. The Wolf King brought you all here from the Other World and taught you to be something you're not. He has been playing with your lives, and life means nothing to him. If you do nothing, you'll join the previous inhabitants of Calendenny and Kevello…in the grave."

Doren cleared his throat and removed his hat. "So now we prepare."

"What will you tell them?" asked Caroline.

"We shall only say that we need to put aside our differences," said Vanaya. "That is all that matters now."

The liberation of Calendenny was accomplished in the early evening after a long session of planning at the safe house. With the help of Doren's well-trained men, the few soldiers of the Wolf King remaining in the village were surprised and subdued before even an alarm could be raised.

"Godspeed, Doren," said Vanaya, as the Dwarf men set off to retake Kevello. Each had been loaned a horse from the Calendenny stables to speed their quest.

"Our people must leave Calendenny as soon as possible," said Garsen. "News of what has transpired here will likely reach the Wolf King before long. We cannot be sitting here idly while his forces over-run us. We will march to the rendezvous point in the Southern Forest as planned and await you there. We must begin the march to Selwys Castle before the sun rises if there is any hope of catching the Wolf King off guard. And even then, it is a faint hope."

"Take care that you're not spied," cautioned Rumil.

"You take care yourself…friend."

Rumil made a face and Garsen laughed.

"Good luck, guys," called Tony as they rode off.

Vanaya turned to Tony.

"Where is Caroline?"

"Oh. She said something about having to do something. She can't have gone far."

"Carith, go find Caroline. Tegwyn, Tony, Garsen, follow me."

Vanaya led them inside the main meeting hall of Calendenny, while all around the folk of Calendenny made preparations. The obelisk sat on a table within.

A black cat leapt onto the table, sniffed the obelisk, and turned away with a disinterested look.

"Shoo, Montgomery Ward," Tegwyn chided. "This is no place for you."

Vanaya chuckled.

"We have a saying," Vanaya said to Tony. "The King's cat only cares about mice."

Tegwyn picked the cat up and deposited him on the floor. Montgomery Ward stalked out of the hall, waving his tail indignantly.

"Tegwyn," said Vanaya, "you must return to the Dwarf safe house. Do you remember the way?"

"What? No! I'm going with you."

"Do not be obstinate, child. We face unknown terrors."

"I'm not afraid. Anyway, I don't remember how to get to the safe house. I would surely lose my way."

"Oh, by the Good...," sputtered Vanaya, annoyed. "We cannot spare Garsen to lead her back. Or you, Tony. We will need your knowledge of the castle grounds."

"Tegwyn will be as safe with us as anywhere," said Garsen, shrugging.

"Then it's decided!" crowed Teglyn. "Let's go then!" She reached for the obelisk.

"No, child!" cried Vanaya.

Tegwyn pulled the obelisk towards herself with one hand across the smooth tabletop. As it reached the edge, she lost her grip and it fell to the floor with a loud crash.

Vanaya gasped. The obelisk lay on its side, inert. After a few seconds, the red light within resumed its steady pulse. Vanaya released her breath.

Tegwyn reached down, picked up and placed the obelisk back on the table. "Oh, to Hell with the *Tylwyth Teg*," she said.

Caroline wandered down the path to Anders Pond alone. The air was now perfectly still and the sounds of the hurried preparations at Calendenny village were faint in the distance, seeming somehow insignificant in the moment. She flung the penny Tegwyn had given her as far as she could into the water, kicked off her shoes, and waded in.

◁ 20 ▷

T he united Elf and Dwarf forces set out from the rendezvous point an hour before sunrise, some on foot, others on horseback. The retaking of Kevello had not gone as smoothly as the liberation of Calendenny, and one of Doren's men, Arno, had suffered a vicious sword wound. Mirta had volunteered to stay behind and look after him, while the remainder of the able-bodied men and women of Kevello and Calendenny were quickly marshaled into a makeshift army armed with bows, swords, hunting knives, wood axes, and assorted farm implements. One of the Elf women raised an improvised battle standard, made from stitched-together bath linens.

Tony and Caroline walked side by side near the head of the assemblage as it made its way across the rolling landscape towards the castle. No signs of pursuit or any reaction from the Wolf King were evident; it was almost disconcertingly quiet. The only sounds were occasional muted birdcalls and the rustle of feet and hooves moving through grass. The morning air was chilly, yet somehow invigorating when drawing breath, as if charged with some electric, eldritch energy.

Caroline turned to Tony.

"Am I supposed to become some kind of butt-kicking, monster-slaying warrior babe now?"

"If we stick close to Rumil and Doren we should be alright. The Wolf King's men aren't real soldiers. They're no different than he is, probably -- just a bunch of nerds playing soldier. Once they realize their weapons are useless they'll surrender. I hope."

"Got any ideas if that dragon shows up?"

"I thought I might try screaming my head off, but I'm not sure if that would help."

"Ha."

Rumil trotted his horse up to Tony's side.

"Not losing your nerve, I trust, Anthony?"

"I'll be okay."

"It was once prophesied at Kevello that two Other Worlders would come to liberate us from the tyranny of the Wolf King."

"Are you being serious?" asked Caroline.

"No. I just thought that I'd say something to bolster your courage. Never mind."

Rumil guided his horse up to a lead position ahead of the army and Tony returned to his morose musings.

"Hold!" commanded Vanaya. "The scout."

A man dressed in Elf camouflage materialized out of the early morning gloom and swiftly walked to the vanguard of the Elf and Dwarf army.

"There is still no sign of enemy activity," he reported. "The land bridge is clear. No army marches out to greet us."

"Could we still have the advantage of surprise?" asked Vanaya.

"That would seem unlikely," replied Doren. "I fear there is somethin' else at play here."

"I tend to agree. We must quicken our pace. The sun will soon arise."

The first rays of the morning sun streaked across the sky as Selwys Castle loomed into view. The pointing claw of rock stood just ahead. The Elves and Dwarves fell into uneasy silence.

"They cannot have failed to have spotted us by now," grumbled Rumil.

"The bridge still stands," observed Vanaya. We must get across before it is dismantled or destroyed."

"Agreed," said Doren. "Rumil, prepare the archers. They need to cover…"

A scream of terror shredded the still morning air.

"What is it?" demanded Vanaya.

"The Ogres! The Ogres!" someone called out. Others gestured in the direction of the triplet hills.

Tony looked but at first could not discern anything unusual. Then something appeared. Something large. Tony realized with a start that it was a huge armored head peering through the gap between the second and third peaks. As the hulking creature climbed into full view, two more Ogres appeared, crossing between the first and second peaks.

"Riders! Archers! Take positions!" ordered Doren.

The first Ogre completed its descent and lumbered with a ponderous, elephantine gait towards the Elf and Dwarf army.

"Oh my God," murmured Caroline.

It towered over fourteen feet. A chainmail cuirass with the Wolf insignia covered its torso, and it wielded a monstrous club. The Ogre was broadly built, with a wide, pumpkin-shaped head covered by a bowl-like helmet, but its features were unmistakably human.

"Remember your instructions," said Doren levelly.

Tony turned to Doren and Vanaya.

"Guys, hold off just a minute. I have a hunch."

"Tony, what are you...?" began Caroline.

Before anyone could say anything further, Tony sprinted out towards the brute.

"Tony!" screamed Caroline.

Tony ran until he was within twenty feet of the creature and stopped. The Ogre stopped as well. Its dark eyes focused on Tony and a rumbling growl escaped its lips. The other two Ogres stopped near the feet of the hills, apparently waiting for their leader to make a move. Tony scanned his surroundings to get his bearings and slowly started backing towards the stone outcropping.

"Everyone hold back!" he cried out.

The Ogre growled more fiercely and advanced as Tony retreated. Tony could see the shadow of the rock outcropping under his feet and knew that he was running out of room.

"He'll be crushed! Do something!" pled Caroline.

Vanaya nodded.

"Garsen, prepare..."

"Wait!" cried Tony, motioning "stop" with his left hand.

He halted, back to the rock outcropping. The Ogre raised its club, and brought it down with frightening violence. Tony leapt backwards at the last minute, crouching at the base of the rock. The club hit the jutting end of the claw...and shattered. The Ogre took a step back, looking surprised and disoriented.

Tony leapt up and sprinted back towards the Elf and Dwarf army.

"It's all right!" he yelled. "Our plan will work!"

"Riders!" called Rumil.

Three horses, each bearing two riders, charged up from the trailing ranks of the army and circled the Ogre. It stood confused, looking from side to side and nervously snarling as the horses galloped around him.

The second rider on the lead horse, an Elf youth named Samus, propped himself up on the saddle and hurled a net at the Ogre. It momentarily entangled the Ogre's right arm, but was flung off. As the Ogre flailed, the horse carrying Samus reared and threw both riders. Another pair of riders charged the monster. A grappling hook was cast up by a Dwarf woman standing fully upright on the stallion's back. It found purchase in the links of the Ogre's armor. The creature roared in surprise and alarm. Samus, not hurt by the fall he had taken, quickly jumped to his feet and seized the end of the rope trailing from the hook.

"Help him! Bring that gollumpus down!" commanded Doren. More Dwarf and Elf men and women ran up to grab the rope. A tug-of-war ensued.

"We need another rope on it!" shouted Rumil. He fastened the end of a line to a heavy ploughshare that Shaw brought up. Grunting with effort, they heaved it up, but it bounced off the titan's thigh. There was a collective gasp as Tegwyn suddenly appeared just beyond reach of the Ogre's flailing arms, picked up the ploughshare and tossed it up. The blade caught neatly on the Ogre's belt.

"Um, yes. That will do," said Rumil.

The Ogre was forced to one knee. Another net flew up, and soon the creature toppled with the force of a demolished building and lay still on the grassy field. Tony could see its face through the mesh. He saw fear.

"Don't hurt him!" yelled Tony. "He's helpless now."

"And the other two are running off," noted Rumil.

"Poor brutes. They were driven by fear, no doubt," said Vanaya. "How did you know, Tony?"

"It was just a hunch, like I said," Tony replied. "He looked winded after that climb. In the "Other World" there was a giant named Robert Wadlow. Not as big as this guy, but really tall, and he never stopped growing during his lifetime. Wadlow got to the point where he could barely stand without assistance; his frame and muscles just weren't strong enough to support his mass. I figured there was a chance the Wolf King might have made the same mistake when he "grew" his Ogres. He probably hoped their size alone would scare off anyone. That club was just for show."

"You scared the crap out of me there, Tony," said Caroline, punching him in the arm.

"Sorry."

"There is still unfinished business here," said Doren. "No time for levity. Secure the Ogre! Prepare to charge the bridge! Quickly!"

"Yes! To the bridge!" echoed Vanaya.

A cry arose from the combined Elf and Dwarf army. Selwys Castle lay just across the bridge.

<svg xmlns="http://www.w3.org/2000/svg"></svg> 21 <svg xmlns="http://www.w3.org/2000/svg"></svg>

Rumil and Garsen charged onto the bridge. Doren stationed himself at a safe distance from the gate to direct the assault while Vanaya cradled the obelisk.

"Shall we knock on the door?" asked Rumil with a twinkle in his eye.

"Hold in the name of the Wolf King!" cried a stern voice. They looked up and saw Karlo standing at the top of the gate.

"Disperse now, or suffer the full unleashed fury of the Wolf King!"

"Do your worst!" retorted Rumil. The other Elves and Dwarves on the bridge jeered.

Karlo held up a pronged lance and pointed it towards Rumil.

"You were warned."

"Yes, yes. Do get on with it, now."

"I said…you were *warned*…"

"Yes, you did say that. Did he say that?"

"He did," agreed Garsen.

"I thought so."

"…that there will be…stern reprisals…"

"Having some problems up there, chap?"

"No! Be quiet, you!"

"I think it's time for you and the Wolf King to listen," challenged Garsen.

"Just…wait!"

Karlo crouched down. Two more Selwys Castle guards, brandishing similar lances, appeared at the top of the gate.

"They're not working!" they heard Karlo explain, flustered. "How are they not working?"

"To the gate!" urged Rumil. Another cry arose and the Elves and Dwarves rushed forward.

"Put your shoulders into it, lads! Where's that ram?"

"Bring up the ram!" ordered Doren. "Make way for the ram!"

Another squad of Elves and Dwarves trotted up the bridge, lugging a pine log with an axe-sharpened end.

"One, two, three, GO!" barked Rumil. The ram, powered by the coordinated effort of nine men and women, crashed into the gate with splintering force.

"Again!"

Tony and Caroline waited next to Vanaya, watching anxiously as the battering ram smashed into the gate repeatedly.

"The gate is starting to shatter!" crowed Rumil triumphantly, turning back to Doren. "I think…"

Rumil suddenly gasped and fell forward. An arrow protruded from his back.

"Archers at the gate! Take cover!" roared Doren.

Tony looked up and saw two of the Wolf King's soldiers armed with bows shooting down at the Elves and Dwarves. Samus blocked another arrow with a small wooden shield he carried, but was knocked off balance and tumbled into the now half-filled ditch.

"Take this child," ordered Vanaya tersely, handing the obelisk to Caroline. Caroline's eyes widened as Vanaya sprinted up to the bridge, bow in hand. In a split second, she knelt, took aim and loosed an arrow at the archer who had shot Rumil. The arrow struck the man in the shoulder and he fell backwards with a cry. The second archer at the gate fell forward into the ditch, as if he had been pushed.

"None of us shot him," said Doren, puzzled.

Tony was relieved to see Rumil stirring. Apparently the arrow had not pierced any vital organs. Rumil groaned and struggled to get to his feet while others restrained him.

"Get the healer over here, quickly," ordered Doren. "An' get Samus out of the water. That Selwys guard too, and tie him up."

A rope was cast down to Samus, who grasped it and shimmied back up. He was still unhurt, remarkably. The Wolf King's archer who had tumbled into the ditch was also dragged out, too soaked and stunned by the fall to offer any resistance. No more soldiers of the Wolf King appeared at the gate.

"What exactly is goin' on over there?" mused Doren.

Crashing sounds, indistinct shouts, and the rumble of trampling feet were heard coming from the other side of the fence. Then abruptly, all was quiet.

"The gate opens!" said Garsen. "Take defensive positions! Move Rumil to safety!"

The Elves and Dwarves pulled back from the gate, weapons held in readiness.

The gate parted with a mechanical hum. A man stepped out.

"*Leutnant* Klemens Korac, Fifth Army, Infantry, Austro-Hungarian Empire," he proclaimed.

"Korac! By the gods, it is Korac!" gasped Doren.

"My children. You have made me proud. Enter and let us stand on the field of victory together."

"Stay close," cautioned Vanaya, as she led Tony, Caroline, and Tegwyn through the gate of Selwys Castle.

A group of the Wolf King's men stood within, held at bay by castle servants wielding farm implements and weapons that they had managed to snatch from guards.

"Once it was clear that their stun weapons were not working, it was a simple matter to take control of the situation," explained Klemens. "We had the element of surprise, after all."

The Dwarves crowded around him in wonder. Tony surveyed the castle grounds. A mare was nervously trotting around the courtyard, warily eyeing the invaders. Two of the Elves ran after it, trying to calm it down. Otherwise, there was no motion or apparent activity.

"We can't let our guard down, here," warned Tony. "I don't think everyone is accounted for."

"Including the Wolf King himself," agreed Vanaya.

"You men," called Klemens, "Let's put these fellows where they cannot trouble us further. That storehouse should do. Get them in there!"

The dispirited guards offered no resistance as Doren's men and the freed servants herded them into the storehouse.

Caroline nudged Tony's shoulder. "Hey look, there's…"

"Endewyn!" cried Vanaya in astonishment.

"Wen?"

It was the turn of the Elves to stare in wonder and cry out in joy.

"The Good Mother! She has returned!"

Wen slowly approached the group, graven faced. She stopped in front of Vanaya. Vanaya bowed her head.

"No, no, dearest. I am the one who should bow and beg for forgiveness."

"You were working for the Wolf King!" said Tony.

"It is true. When the first Calendenny perished, I was given the task of restoring it. I chose Vanaya to be the leader after she was brought to us from a land of unforgiving winter. I knew that she could adapt, survive, lead. I did not choose wrong."

"I do not understand, Mother," said Vanaya, weeping.

"You taught the Elves and Dwarves to hate each other!" accused Caroline.

"I swear I did not. The Wolf King's men fostered this hatred in them. I taught my children to ignore differences, overcome barriers. The stories I told you…remember, my children? Everything I did with the best of intentions. But I fell into the Wolf King's trap, and all my dreams were twisted into something evil. I should have listened to my mother. She always said that the greatest sin enters through the smallest door."

"What happened to the first Calendenny? And Kevello?" demanded Tony.

"Hold on, boy," said Klemens, interposing himself between Wen and Tony. "You do not understand everything that has happened here."

"That's why I'm asking," retorted Tony, angrily.

"I would know as well," said Garsen, stepping up.

"There will be time for explanations, but it is not now," said Wen, with sudden urgency in her voice. "Klemens! They have taken her! He has taken her!"

"Who?"

"Monique!"

"Oh no!" said Caroline.

"We will enter the Wolf's den and get her back," said Klemens. "Doren, lad! Gather your strongest men. Have no fear, Wen, we will..."

At first Tony thought that a bomb had been set off. Klemens collapsed to the ground without uttering a further word.

"Get down!" hissed Tony at Caroline and Tegwyn. "In there!"

Tony led them into the guard booth next to the gate. The Elves, Dwarves, and castle servants searched for the source of the attack, holding their weapons and shields in readiness.

"Look!" said Caroline.

Someone stepped from behind one of the guard barracks. It was Gerard, holding a handgun.

"Well, it seems your magic doesn't stop 45 caliber bullets. I don't know how you conjured your mischief and I don't care. It is time for this petty exercise in peasant revolt to end. I suggest that you withdraw your forces from the castle grounds. Put that bow down, you. Hiram! Matthias!"

Two more of the Wolf King's guards stepped forward, each armed with a pistol.

"The Wolf King likes tradition. I like security. It's what I was hired for. Now start putting down those nasty sharp things, and you may walk out of here unharmed if you cooperate. But quickly!"

Doren and Vanaya looked at each other. Tony could hear his pulse pounding in his ears.

"Dwarves!" said Doren. "Take these men down!"

An arrow flew towards Gerard, but he narrowly dodged it and dropped to the ground. He pointed his pistol at Doren and fired. There was a flash and the sound of a ricochet. The space in the courtyard between the combined Elf and Dwarf forces and the Wolf King's private guard glowed, shimmered. Swirling lights from all ranges of the color spectrum blazed out in all directions.

"Hey, that's..." began Tony.

"A time ship!" finished Caroline.

"Attention!" blared a woman's voice. "Temporal Affairs has now assumed control of this compound! All combatants are ordered to immediately put down their weapons and surrender."

The time shuttle fully materialized in the center of the courtyard. Its hatches swung open and three men in dark uniforms emerged.

"Doren! Vanaya! Tell your people to stand down!" yelled Tony from the guard booth.

Doren nodded. "Lower your weapons!" he commanded.

"Drop those guns!" ordered one of the Temporal Affairs Agents.

A shot rang out.

"They're still firing! Take defensive positions!"

The Temporal Affairs Agents crouched down next to the shuttle. One drew something that looked like a fountain pen from a pocket. He pointed it towards the storehouse that Gerard had ducked behind. There was a brief pulse of light and the sound of a muffled explosion.

"They're all hiding among those shacks. Set for Level 3 concuss," instructed the lead Temporal Affairs Agent. He turned back towards the Elves, Dwarves, and castle servants. "You people move away from the combat zone. Keep your heads low!"

Tony moved closer to the door of the guard booth.

"Tony, what are you doing?" asked Caroline.

"I've got to get to Monique."

"Are you mental? Those guys out there have guns."

"There are enough bodies between us. And that time shuttle besides. I have to try. We can't leave Monique in the hands of the Wolf King."

"How about we leave it to the professionals?"

"They've got their hands full. You stay here, Caroline."

Tony poked his head out, saw that the path was clear, and headed for the main keep.

"Tony!"

The Wolf King's security guards and the Temporal Affairs Agents were exchanging fire with increasing intensity.

"You stay here, Tegwyn," said Caroline, and ran after Tony.

❧ 22 ❧

Tony sprinted up the path, quickly turning his head to survey the situation in the courtyard. The Elves, Dwarves and castle servants were still pinned down by fire from the Wolf King's private guard. Some, including Vanaya and Doren, had taken cover behind the time shuttle, others crouched or lay behind what cover there was available on the castle grounds: animal pens, a broken-down wagon, stables. There was a foray by a small group of Dwarves toward the storehouses the Wolf King's guards were holed up in, but it didn't get far; the headstrong leader of the charge went down under fire and the others retreated. One of the Temporal Affairs men was able to drag the wounded Dwarf back to safety under the cover fire of the other Agents. The flurry of fire and counter-fire must have kept the private guard's attention focused on the Agents, because Tony was able to reach the entrance without being targeted.

Tony hopped up the stone steps and into the foyer. He paused to let his eyes adjust to the dark. None of the torches on the wall were lit, so it was even darker than he remembered. He saw no one, but there were distant sounds of running feet and a heavy door being closed. He heard footsteps behind him and whirled around. It was Caroline and Tegwyn.

"Tony! What do you think you're doing?"

"You girls stay here. I have to stop the Wolf King."

"You don't have any way to fight him."

"I'll figure something out I guess."

"Well, I'm not staying behind."

"Neither am I," said Tegwyn, obstinately.

159

Tony rolled his eyes.

"Okay, stay close, then. I'm guessing he took her to his courtroom. I heard something going on back there. Let's go. But quietly!"

"Alright. And I saw you roll your eyes, buster."

They crept down the hall. There were no further sounds of activity. Their pace grew slower as they anxiously approached the entrance to the courtroom. Abruptly there was a loud creaking. Someone was opening the door.

"Split up!" said Tony. He opened one of the side doors and gestured at the one across the hall. Caroline nodded in understanding and she and Tegwyn scurried into the room at the opposite side of the hall. Tony closed the door behind him and pressed against it. He heard the thick oaken door of the courtroom creak closed and then the sound of someone walking quickly down the hallway. He released his breath as the steps faded away.

"Well, I must say this is quite a surprise, Tony Marco," said a mocking voice behind him.

Tony recognized the voice immediately. It was Gaudet.

Caroline and Tegwyn closed the door behind them and heard the footsteps pass. Caroline turned around to examine the room they were in. She gasped.

"Oh my God!"

"What is it, Caroline?"

The tiles shined. An ornate round mirror hung over a marble sink. The smell of various exotically scented soaps and shampoos filled the room. A claw-toe bathtub sat behind a translucent curtain hanging from the ceiling, and a porcelain commode adorned with a vase and flowers completed the tableau.

"It's...a bathroom! An honest-to-God bathroom!"

Gaudet marched Tony down the hall, his two-pronged lance pointed at the small of Tony's back.

"This will knock you right out if it connects," he warned.

Gaudet stopped at the last door on the left before the courtroom. "In there."

Tony opened the door and walked in with Gaudet right behind him.

Sir Penultimate Theorem stood behind a desk adorned only with an antiquated desktop computer and reading lamp.

"What the...? Gaudet! What's going on?"

"It seems we've got a bit of a revolution on our hands."

"The Agents are here, aren't they? We've got to get out of here. Where did this one come from? Isn't he the one that escaped last week?"

"The Agents will have their hands full for a while if the Wolf King's private guard has anything to say about it. I caught this one trying to sneak in. Up to no good I expect. Maybe we can have a little fun before we abscond?"

Sir Penultimate Theorem smiled crookedly.

"Well, I didn't appreciate this one's attitude."

He walked up to Tony, sneering.

"This is going to be bad, Old Timer."

"Count on it," said Tony.

Gaudet's lance was suddenly pointed squarely at Sir Penultimate Theorem's solar plexus. His eyes widened.

"What do you think you're doing, Gaudet?"

"You just be still now, hear?"

Tony quickly searched the room. Another lance and some familiar looking metallic boots were stored in an open closet.

"I think these are just what I need," he said to Gaudet. "Show me how they work."

Gaudet stepped up to the courtroom door, paused for a second and listened.

"Keep your guard up," he cautioned Tony.

He thrust the door open.

"Inside," he ordered Sir Penultimate Theorem, gesturing with his lance. Within, the Wolf King stood, his back to the door, studying a screen mounted in the far wall displaying images from the conflict in the courtyard. The Wolf King whirled in surprise.

"Gaudet, what's going on here?"

"Wolf King!" yelled Sir Penultimate Theorem, "Gaudet's turned on us!"

"Well?" asked the Wolf King.

"I found this one sneaking about," said Gaudet, nodding at Tony.

"Wolf King! Listen! He's turned traitor!"

Gaudet turned to Tony and nodded.

"Why aren't you listening to me?" pleaded Sir Penultimate Theorem.

The Wolf King took a few steps forward, squinting at Gaudet's captive.

"Say, isn't that the…"

Just then, Gaudet raised his lance and fired a blinding blast at the Wolf King. The Wolf King tried to dive out of the way, but the blast clipped him and he crumpled to the floor.

Gaudet turned to Sir Penultimate Theorem, shaking and cowering at his side.

"Looks like he had you on ignore," said Gaudet. He jammed his lance into the young man's stomach. Sir Penultimate Theorem convulsed and fell in a heap.

"Guard!" cried the Wolf King from his knees on the floor.

A man emerged from a door at the rear of the courtroom and charged Tony and Gaudet, brandishing his own lance. Gaudet leapt in front of Tony. The guard and Gaudet collided with a shuddering impact and a sound of crackling energy. Both of the lances found their respective targets and both men fell senseless onto the floor. Tony saw the guard's face clearly for the first time and recognized him as the man called Farlowe.

The Wolf King cursed and got to his feet.

"What have you done with Monique?" Tony demanded, raising the lance he had taken from Sir Penultimate Theorem's office. He shifted his feet. The boots seemed heavy and clunky. Had he been mistaken in putting them on?

"The girl is already down with the Drake. I'd suggest you back off now or I'll loose the beast on her."

"Let it have me instead. You don't want to hurt that girl."

"Well, I was just going to kill you myself. But why not let the Drake have you both?"

The Wolf King retrieved his own lance and raised it. Blinding light surged from its tip. The power of the obelisk was either spent or of no effect within the castle. Tony immediately leapt, and found himself hurtling across the courtroom directly at the Wolf King. He had misjudged the power of the Lift Boots. The Wolf King ducked out of the way. Tony collided with the heavy wooden throne and knocked it over. The Wolf King also misjudged his leap, flew into a fireplace on one side of the courtroom and bounced backwards, cursing as he fell. Tony stood up, aimed his lance, and pressed the firing control. The Wolf King rolled out of the way of the blast, and while still rolling, fired another volley at Tony. Tony pressed the "shield" control on the lance and the Wolf King's shot was deflected. Tony leapt to the center of the courtroom in one bound. The Wolf King regained his feet and aimed a blast at the candle chandelier hanging from the middle of the ceiling. It rattled and collapsed to the floor, but missed Tony.

Tony aimed another shot at his opponent, but the Wolf King deflected it easily.

"Not getting anywhere here," Tony said to himself under his breath. He looked down at the floor, carefully positioning himself.

"Tony!" Caroline screamed.

He looked back over his shoulder and saw Caroline and Tegwyn standing at the doorway. He lowered his lance. The Wolf King aimed and fired. Tony vanished in a blaze of light.

$\approx$ **23** $\approx$

C aroline screamed. The Wolf King turned towards her. Gaudet
struggled to his feet and recovered his lance.

"You back off now," he warned, closing on the Wolf King.

The Wolf King snarled at Gaudet but turned and retreated through
the door at the rear of the courtroom, closing it behind him.

"Come on! We have to follow him," said Gaudet to Caroline.
"Tony's still alive, down there somewhere. It was a trap door."

Caroline backed away, motioning Tegwyn to follow her.

"It's okay, Caroline sweetheart. I'm on your side. I swear."

He stamped his feet on the panel where Tony had stood moments
before.

"I think the Wolf King's lance has the only control. But we can still
get down there by a stairway."

Gaudet quickly strode across the courtroom to the rear door. It was
unlocked and he entered, with Caroline and Tegwyn following at a
cautious distance. Through the door was a small study where Neon
Sparrow sat behind a desk piled with stacks of thick, yellowed books.

"He's gone. Through there," Neon Sparrow said in a resigned tone,
gesturing at metallic elevator-style doors next to a bookcase.

Gaudet inspected the doors. There were no obvious controls.

"How do you open it?" he demanded.

"Voice command code."

"What is it?"

"I don't know."

"You're lying."

"I couldn't hear it. He whispered."

165

Gaudet pointed his lance at Neon Sparrow. She stared back, impassionate.

"Wait," said Caroline. "Court Reporter. Play back Wolf King's statements. Past five minutes."

Nothing happened.

Neon Sparrow sighed. "Court Reporter. Play back Wolf King's statements. Past five minutes."

"1 November, 1098, 8:47 A.M., Wolf King: *They're coming! Don't you care anymore?* [Intervening comment by Neon Sparrow] Wolf King: *Yeah? Well, I hope they throw you into the temporal void, you* [expletive deleted]. *Lemuria.*"

The doors slid open, revealing stone steps leading downward.

"Well, let's go," said Caroline.

The force of the Wolf King's blast had stunned Tony, but he managed not to black out. He slid down a steep ramp in near total darkness, then tumbled head-over-heels onto a damp, dirt surface. He found himself in a wide chamber, some sort of basement, with twenty-foot high smooth stone walls. Torches were mounted on the walls, equidistantly positioned around the chamber. As his eyes adjusted, he saw Monique huddled against the wall on the far side of the chamber. The Drake was there – over twenty feet long, thick crocodilian tale, short snout, large protruding ridges over its eyes. It was still, but clearly had its attention focused on the girl.

Tony realized that he no longer had his lance; it must have fallen out of his grasp during his slide down into the basement and gotten stuck somewhere. He had to act fast. He ran to a spot beneath one of the torches. It was about fifteen feet up. Tony leapt straight up, grabbed the torch out of its metallic holder, and managed to keep his balance upon landing. Then he sprung across the room to a point halfway between Monique and the Drake. He waved the torch at the monstrous reptile.

"Monique! Run! *Corre!*"

Monique was clearly terrified. She looked helplessly back at Tony and shook her head. The Drake was obviously agitated now, swiveling its massive armored head from side to side, seeming to inflate itself to even more monstrous proportions. Monique finally mustered her courage and fled to the far side of the chamber. The Drake turned away from Tony and crept towards the girl. Tony leapt after it, landing behind it. He bashed the massive, armored tail, employing the torch as a club. The Drake's tail swung away and then crashed back like a pendulum into Tony. He was thrown ten feet back against the far wall, and collapsed senselessly. The torch fell out of his hand. The Drake turned towards Tony.

Caroline ran down the stone steps, with Tegwyn and Gaudet following close behind. The steps led to an observation platform overlooking a wide stone chamber. The Wolf King stood there, looking down at a nightmare tableau: Tony Marco lying helplessly on the ground and the monstrous, hissing Drake stalking his still form. Caroline gasped.

The Wolf King turned.

"You again! I never should have trusted Neon Sparrow."

"You call that monster off!" Caroline said, running up to him.

"You honestly think I can control it?" the Wolf King replied with a laugh.

"Step aside, girl" said Gaudet, brandishing his lance.

"Gaudet, *et tu*. I can't count on anyone, can I?" He raised his own lance defensively.

Gaudet fired a blast at the Wolf King, but he deflected it with a bored look. The Wolf King pointed his lance at Caroline and Tegwyn.

"Behind me, girls!" said Gaudet, charging at the Wolf King. He deflected the Wolf King's shot and ploughed into him. Gaudet and the Wolf King grappled. Gaudet pinned the Wolf King's arms to his side in a bear hug. The Wolf King struggled, pulled one arm free and pressed the end of his lance into Gaudet's torso. Gaudet fell, dropping his lance. It hit the ground and rolled toward Caroline. She picked it up.

"Tegwyn, get clear," she said.

Tegwyn took several steps sideways.

The Wolf King laughed.

"Too easy," he said. He pointed his lance at Caroline. Tegwyn sprang at the Wolf King. Caught off guard, the Wolf King fired a wild, off-balance shot that went between the two girls. Caroline stepped up and jammed Gaudet's lance into the Wolf King's chest. His hair stood up, his eyes dilated and he toppled backwards, over the rail of the observation platform, down onto the basement floor.

Tony shook his head, trying to regain his senses. The whole right side of his body, which had borne the brunt of the swipe of the Drake's tail, was in pain. He saw that Monique had retrieved the fallen torch and was waving it and calling out, trying to get the Drake's attention.

"No, Monique!" he yelled.

There was a sudden dull thud. Tony turned and saw the Wolf King sprawled senselessly on the ground on the far side of the chamber. The Drake seemed to lose interest in Tony and Monique and lumbered towards the unconscious Wolf King.

Tony heard Caroline's voice coming from above.

"Tony!" she called. Then in an alarmed tone, "Tegwyn, what are you doing?"

Tony looked up and saw Tegwyn climbing over a rail at the top of the wall. She grasped the railing with both hands, hung from it momentarily and then let go and fell to the floor, landing on her feet. She turned to the Drake. Tony stumbled forward, but found he could barely walk. Tegwyn stood directly before the Drake and began humming and singing softy. The Drake hissed and continued to look agitated, pivoting its head from side to side.

"Tegwyn! Get away from that thing!" yelled Caroline from above.

Tegwyn stood her ground and continued to sing, her voice growing louder, bolder.

"And did she wear wild flowers in her hair?"

The Drake's head stopped swaying and lowered. It lay on the ground in front of Tegwyn, now completely docile and motionless.

Tony then heard an unfamiliar woman's voice.

"Get them out of there," the woman said.

168

❧ 24 ☙

Tony looked up again and saw one of the Temporal Affairs Agents and Doren tossing a net down over the railing.

"Grab it, Tony. We'll pull you up."

"First the girls!" shouted Tony. Tegwyn and Monique each took a hold of the net and were hauled up to the observation platform. Another net was cast down for Tony. The Temporal Affairs Agent climbed down and collected the Wolf King, now conscious again but stunned and not struggling. The Drake continued to lie still on the basement floor.

Caroline hugged Tony as soon as he had clambered onto the observation platform.

"Tony, you are a complete nut. What were you thinking?"

"I was pretty sure about the trap door from the start. I knew that the Wolf King's staff didn't disintegrate Farlowe. It's just a glorified toy, not too different from what we saw in the Time Station arcade. In fact Mr. Gaudet and I ran into Farlowe in the courtroom a few minutes ago. He must have been a plant in the worker's camp. I guess that whole scene when we arrived was just staged to scare us into submission."

"But what about the dragon?"

"I didn't have any idea of what I was getting myself into there, admittedly. But then I got a look at it. Look, Caroline! Don't you recognize it? From Mr. Wolski's science class? Uromastyx! A vegetarian lizard!"

"Vegetarian? But how could you be sure?"

"Well, I guess I couldn't. Who knows what the Wolf King did to it. And it could have crushed Monique with its tail easily, if it were mad enough. I guess we were all lucky."

"And that Tegwyn…"

"Tegwyn!" cried Vanaya, emerging from the stairs onto the observation platform. She embraced Tegwyn warmly. Monique stood nearby, looking a bit lost.

The Temporal Affairs Agent, Doren, and Garsen stood guard over Sir Penultimate Theorem, Farlowe and the Wolf King, now all held in wrist restraints. A tall brunette woman in a Temporal Affairs uniform stood before Gaudet, whose hands were now restrained as well.

Another male Agent came down the stairs.

"Report," directed the female Agent in a stern monotone.

"The last hostile has been subdued. Situation normalized. One confirmed casualty, male, mid 60's…"

"Klemens," murmured Tony regretfully.

"…several others wounded, three seriously. Agent Robinson has begun administering first aid."

"Return and assist Robinson," ordered the woman.

"Understood, Agent Savoy."

"Well, Gloria," said Gaudet in a mock conversational tone, "You're looking stunning as usual."

"Quiet. And it's Agent Savoy to you. Furthermore this is certainly no time for levity. Temp Affairs is prepared to file some serious charges against you, including possible complicity in the mass murder of the previous inhabitants of this so-called kingdom."

"There was no murder, I swear. The old Kevello, Calendenny -- clones cooked up in the Wolf King's lab."

"But still human, regardless of their genesis!"

"Absolutely, but they were not murdered. Wolfgang was just beginning his genetic experiments at the time, learning as he dabbled. He was able to alter their features to make them look more like creatures from fairy stories, but they were genetically infirm. They all died, one after the other, ultimately."

"That's horrible!" cried Caroline.

"That it was, child," agreed Gaudet in a more somber tone. "That's why I convinced Wolfgang to repopulate his kingdom another way. I did my part to reduce casualties by bringing in people rescued from dire straits in their own time, like that little girl."

He nodded at Monique.

"I can't speak for the others who did Wolfgang's dirty work. I suspect they were less concerned about such things."

"Hmm," murmured Agent Savoy in a dubious tone.

"And that's why I brought Tony and Caroline here. Wolfgang thought that I had kidnapped them out of the early 21st Century. He didn't know that they had been through the Khronos-Solarin Time Station and would eventually be traced back here."

"So you're saying you brought us here on purpose?" asked Tony, incredulously.

"Exactly that. And I never suspected you were planning a fool escape. I had to lead the Wolf King's men on a wild goose chase out to the Mongrahan Hills to throw them off your trail. If you two had just stayed put the Agents would have tracked you here eventually."

"What about Tegwyn? What's her story?" asked Caroline, now stepping forward to confront Gaudet.

"She was a prototype. For the next generation."

"Does that mean she's going to...?"

"Die? No, I don't think so. The Wolf King learned from his mistakes."

"So that's why the Wolf King didn't want the Elves and Dwarves to have children."

"Correct, Caroline. It was a simple matter utilizing late 21st Century medicine to introduce birth control agents via their food supply."

"But if there was another generation of clones coming, where would they fit in?" asked Tony.

"One way or another, there was going to be a war to make room for the new generation of Elves and Dwarves."

"The Wolf King wanted Calendenny and Kevello to destroy each other!" cried Vanaya in disgust. "We discerned his plotting in time, with help from Tony and Caroline."

Gaudet nodded.

"That's why I knew I had to act, and quickly. When I spied Tony and Caroline on the Time Station, I saw my opportunity."

"Yet, you could have just come straight to Temporal Affairs and confessed," pointed out Agent Savoy reproachfully.

"I was hoping I could avoid the whole "surrendering to Temporal Affairs" scenario. I've been down that road before, you see."

"Unbelievable," said Agent Savoy. "Well, I guess you'll have your opportunity to tell your side of the story to the Temporal Affairs tribunal."

"And what's going to happen to us?" asked Caroline. "And the servants? The Elves and Dwarves?"

"The people kidnapped by the Wolf King will be repatriated to their own places of origin and native time frames."

"But Monique was rescued by Gaudet from a mob that was trying to kill her! And what about Tegwyn? And those poor Ogres and the Drake?"

Agent Savoy looked flustered.

"A complete investigation of what damage has been done here must be conducted before I can even consider what recommendation I give Temporal Affairs."

"Agent Savoy!" interrupted the remaining male Agent, "These prisoners have sufficiently recovered so that they can be moved. May I escort them to the shuttle?"

"Proceed," responded Agent Savoy. "I can handle things from here."

The Wolf King glared at Tony as he was led out, flanked by the Agent. Tony stepped in front of his path.

"You have things I could only dream of in my time -- underwater cities, time stations, miraculous advances in science and medicine. You could have and do so much, but all you did was wreck a bunch of peoples' lives. And for what? For fun because you're bored?"

The Wolf King looked at Tony as if seeing him for the first time. He leaned forward and said something. The Agent prodded him and the prisoners were escorted back up the stone steps.

Caroline walked up to Tony.

"I heard what you said. That was pretty cool. But what did he answer? It sounded like *I'll remember you.*"

"No," answered Tony. "I think he said, *I remember you.*"

Caroline turned to Agent Savoy again.

"So, what about us, then?"

"You'll have to remain in custody of Temporal Affairs while we sort out everything that happened here."

"But we're innocent here! And we helped you nab your guy."

"Nevertheless, we need to ascertain everything that has transpired here as accurately as possible. We'll need detailed statements from you for starters."

"And then a lesson in the ethics of time travel, eh? Which I violated by saving that little girl in 15th Century Spain, I should point out," added Gaudet with a smirk.

"What does he mean?" asked Caroline.

"Any interference with past lives and events is viewed with the strictest scrutiny under the Time Travel Code."

"Monique would have died," said Tony.

"Possibly. If there had been no interference from the future she would have died hundreds of years ago in our timeframe, regardless. Whatever the case, we cannot become the arbiters of who will live and die."

"But that's not how it works," protested Caroline. "That's *never* how it works! If there's someone who is in trouble, you help them!"

"It's never that simple," replied Agent Savoy dismissively.

"You know what I think? I don't think you people can claim moral superiority to the Wolf King and his goons. You've turned time travel into a leisure activity for bored rich people from the future, but you wouldn't lift a finger to help a little girl..."

"Caroline..." broke in Tony.

"You back off, Tony! This is making me so angry."

"I appreciate that you've been through a lot," said Agent Savoy.

"Don't patronize me."

"Agent Savoy," said Tony, "We'll cooperate with Temporal Affairs. We just want to know that our friends here will be safe."

"The interference has already occurred and has been woven into history. As for the girl, even if we could ascertain exactly when and where she came from we would not now return her to a perilous situation."

"I cannot be parted from my dear Tegwyn," broke in Vanaya. "I'd sooner die."

"And I would never be parted from Vanaya," added Garsen.

"Where would be the morality in breaking up a family?" sneered Gaudet.

"I told you to hold your tongue, Stephen," warned Agent Savoy. "I...hold on, I'm getting a call. Go ahead, Robinson."

She took several steps away and began a muted conversation.

"I could get you two back to Corpus Christi with no questions asked," whispered Gaudet to Tony and Caroline when Agent Savoy had turned away. "The Wolf King has a shuttle hidden here. I know where it is."

"Yeah, as if we'd trust you now," said Tony scornfully.

"I promised you and Caroline on my honor that I would get you home safe and sound. These Temp Affairs people ain't going to let you go anytime soon. You've seen too much of their operation. They're in an awkward position."

"Back away from the prisoner," said Agent Savoy, swiftly walking back towards them.

"Agent Savoy," asked Tony. "Can you give us a time frame of when we would be allowed to return to our homes? Our time?"

"It's really not my call. Like I said, you'd have to be fully debriefed, and we have to ascertain the full extent of the damage done here and what crimes might have been committed. Assuming there are no complications, it could still be months."

"Months!" cried Caroline. "To Hell with that. I've had enough of this now!"

She spied something at Vanaya's feet.

"Vanaya!" Caroline called, nodding at the floor.

Vanaya crouched down, picked up the Wolf King's fallen lance and tossed it to Caroline. Before Agent Savoy could act to defend herself, Caroline stuck the prongs of the lance into her shoulder. Savoy fell, groaning.

Gaudet laughed cruelly.

"Can you really get us out of here? Now?" asked Caroline.

"Sure thing, Miss Caroline."

"Caroline, are you sure this is a good idea?" asked Tony.

"I'm not taking any chances."

She pointed the lance directly at Gaudet's head.

"One false move and this goes straight into your skull and I don't remove it until your brain is completely fried. Understood?"

Gaudet turned to Tony.

"I'm pretty sure she's not bluffing," said Tony.

"I'm quite satisfied that she is not," agreed Gaudet.

"Take us!" pled Vanaya urgently. "Return us to my country in the Other World. I will return to my old life and Garsen and I will raise Tegwyn as our daughter, as we have in this world."

"What about Monique?" asked Tegwyn.

"I don't trust these Temporal Affairs creeps," said Caroline. "They'll probably just drop her off back where she came from, alone and unprotected."

"She can come with us!" said Tegwyn, her face lit with anticipation.

"Oh, but we're forgetting something," said Tony, sober disappointment in his voice. "People are "tethered" to their own time, as Mr. Gaudet put it. If Tegwyn returns with Vanaya she'll just get swooped back to the 11th Century."

"Not necessarily, Mr. Tony," said Gaudet with a gleam in his eye. "You see, Tegwyn was born here, in the Wolf King's Temporal Proprietary, within a temporal stasis bubble. In a very real sense, she has no native time stream because none attached to her. She can move freely within time without fear of being swooped."

"Really? That's incredible. But what do we do about Garsen and Monique? Monique was born in the 15th Century, and I think Garsen came from the late 20th Century."

"I have one more lifeline," responded Gaudet.

"Well?" demanded Caroline.

"The Wolf King's time shuttle is equipped with a personal temporal stasis device, for special situations when someone has to venture beyond the field generated by the shuttle. It's worn on the wrist, self-charging via solar power, and could function indefinitely in theory. Even in a land of midnight sun."

"One?"

"Just one, I'm afraid."

"Give it to the girl," said Garsen.

"Oh, Garsen," said Caroline, shaking her head slowly.

"My darling," Vanaya gasped.

"It must be done to keep the girl safe. I will return to my time and place content in the knowledge that my beloved Vanaya and Tegwyn are safe and together somewhere."

Vanaya kissed Garsen tearfully.

"I will never forget you, beloved."

"Maybe we shall meet again, if yet in another world."

Tegwyn turned to Monique.

"Would you like to be my sister?"

Monique took Tegwyn's outstretched hand.

"Yes," she said.

Caroline turned to Tony in surprise.

"She can speak English!"

Tegwyn laughed.

"Very well. Now that that's settled, everyone who wants to go, come with me now," said Gaudet, impatiently.

"Doren?" asked Tony.

"It's been a pleasure makin' your acquaintance, Tony and Caroline. And yours, Vanaya."

"Okay, you two run on ahead and delay the Agents if they return," Gaudet instructed Doren and Garsen. "And someone please release my hands. I'll be needing them."

"Bless you, Doren," said Vanaya. "Farewell, my beloved Garsen. If you see the others from Calendenny, tell them what became of us."

Garsen embraced Tegwyn and kissed Vanaya one final time. Doren half bowed. "Farewell an' good luck to you all," he said and quickly ran back up the stairs.

❧ 25 ❧

E ndewyn Celeste Vaughn was born on April 21, 1920 on a family farm in Montgomeryshire County in Wales. Her parents, Owen and Sian were Catholic, and had Endewyn fairly late in life, the only child of their marriage. Endewyn's aunt Rhian, eleven years younger than Sian, assumed the role of an elder sister to the girl. As a young girl, Endewyn admired crooner Donald Peers and displayed an early aptitude for dance. She dreamed of one day appearing on stage in Cardiff, or even London. At bedtime, Aunt Rhian entertained Endewyn with folk tales about the fair people who lived in the mountains, learned in turn from her own mother. As Endewyn grew to adolescence, it became increasingly clear that she had been blessed with great beauty. Aunt Rhian often teased her about being a changeling child of the *Tylwyth Teg*. Endewyn was not overly impressed with the suitors that eventually called at her door, most of whom she had known since childhood, others who had been awkwardly introduced at social events by her mother.

In the fall of 1937, Endewyn and Rhian visited relatives in Swansea. It was there, as she and her aunt strolled along a line of shops, that Endewyn met Edward. Edward was a slight young man, shy and self-effacing, who worked on piers unloading cargo ships. Endewyn was immediately smitten, and with the cooperation of Rhian soon made her feelings clear to him. After that, Edward called upon Endewyn regularly during the time she was in Swansea. Edward and Endewyn would sit looking out over the bay as the sun set, chatting oblivious to the world around for so long that Rhian was often obliged to fetch Endewyn and return her to their relatives' house. Edward promised

Endewyn, on the eve of her return to the family farm, that he would present himself to her parents and sue for her hand in marriage.

Edward was true to his word, but he balked when he learned that Endewyn's family was Catholic. His own family devoutly adhered to the Church in Wales, and strongly disapproved of marriage outside the Church. Endewyn, deflated, sulked in her room and shunned the company of people for months afterward. Only upon urging from Rhian did she finally emerge, and resolved to find Edward and make him realize his folly. With her parents' blessing, she returned to Swansea the following year. She found Edward still working on the docks. He tried to ignore Endewyn at first, but she returned every day, telling jokes, singing songs and on one occasion, dancing a fiery jig to the delight of all of the stevedores present. After several weeks of this, Edward could no longer deny the stirrings in his heart. Risking the opprobrium he faced from his parents, Edward finally asked for Endewyn's hand in marriage. They were wed on Christmas Eve in 1938.

When war broke out in Europe, Edward joined the Merchant Navy and quickly rose in rank to a boatswain on a Fyffes Line freighter. The war years were a time of great personal stress for Endewyn, relieved only on the occasions when Edward safely returned from a successful run. After the war ended, Edward retired from the Merchant Navy to spend more time with his wife. Endewyn rejoiced and looked forward to raising a family with Edward. However, the seasons passed and the young couple was not blessed with a child. A visit to a doctor confirmed unwelcome news: Endewyn was incapable of having children of her own. Edward and Endewyn were both distraught.

Soon after that misfortune, Edward accepted an offer from a wartime shipmate to join what was promised to be a lucrative merchant run to Jamaica. Endewyn's worst fears were realized when it was reported that Edward was lost when the freighter ran aground on rocks off Anglesey. Endewyn returned to the family farm and spent the next several years caring for her parents, both aging and ailing by this time. Her mother passed away in 1948 and her father succumbed to illness the following year. By this time, Rhian had married an American serviceman and departed overseas with him. Endewyn continued to operate the farm with the help of hired hands. Care aged her prematurely and her once girlish figure was rounded by the years. She shunned contact with others increasingly. Endewyn had been proud of her ability to attract men in her youth and was particularly disillusioned by her perceived loss of beauty.

Endewyn met the American named Gaudet one day while trudging up a hill, searching for a wayward ewe. She accepted his company readily enough once she realized that he was not interested in her romantically. However, after several hours of lively conversation over tea and biscuits, Gaudet did stun her with a remarkable proposition. He told her that she could become a real mother, and care for a whole village of children. Gaudet told her to consider it and answer him when he returned in one week. Despite the fantastic elements of his story, Endewyn accepted when Gaudet returned the following Sunday.

Gaudet presented Endewyn to the Wolf King, who agreed that she could be one of the genetic mothers of the children of Calendenny. Although she was never told, it was clear that the child she named Vanaya, one of the first children born, was hers by the strange method of reproduction that the Wolf King called cloning. She rapturously raised Vanaya and her "siblings," doted on them, and called them the candle of her eye. The Wolf King entrusted her to be the main caretaker of all of them, although other servants of the Wolf King would assist her when needed. Endewyn's heart broke again when the "Elven" children, just passing into adolescence, all sickened and died. She demanded that the Wolf King return her to Wales, but he refused, and said that there would be more children. Endewyn refused to donate more genetic material, but the Wolf King told her that it would not be necessary.

Endewyn was plotting her next move when Gaudet arrived with the fair-haired child Vendela. Endewyn's heart was instantly won over by the ragged waif from northern lands, and took the child into her care. There were no further protests when the other children arrived, ferried in by Gaudet and other servants of the Wolf King from distant places and times. Endewyn taught Vendela English and, in accordance with the wishes of the Wolf King, led all the children to believe that they were kin of the fairy folk from the stories of her childhood. Naturally enough, she soon began calling the fair-haired girl Vanaya.

Many of the things that Endewyn had seen in the Wolf King's strange kingdom gave her pause and made her lie awake at night. Yet it seemed as if the Almighty had now given her another chance to fulfill her dream of raising a family. The Croatian ex-soldier Klemens Korac, newly arrived to provide a father figure to the new children of Kevello, soon became a frequent, if furtive, companion. Officially, the Wolf King discouraged contact between the Elf and Dwarf camps.

As the children grew to adolescence and became increasingly self-sufficient, she was instructed by the Wolf King's servants to leave them to their own devices. As uneasy as this prospect made her, she had no choice but to obey the Wolf King's wishes, as she knew that dire reprisal would follow disobedience. Endewyn was permitted a brief return to Calendenny to present the girl Tegwyn, a prototype of a new generation of clones, to Vanaya. Endewyn returned to Selwys Castle, along with Klemens, to assume a supervisory position among the castle servants, awaiting the next return of the Wolf King. She took the new servants under her wing as they arrived at the castle, confused and frightened. She named the little Spanish girl Monique, a name she had always found exotic and beautiful.

When the Temporal Affairs agents raided Selwys Castle and rounded up the Wolf King's cohorts, Endewyn was taken into custody. After an inquiry, it was decided to absolve her of any crimes and release her to her own native time. She was returned to Swansea in the year 1995, as she was now seventy-five years old. She located some of her still-living relatives in that city, who took her in.

One day late in the year 2004, Endewyn's relatives were surprised to receive an American man and a strikingly beautiful white-haired woman named Vanaya, come all the way from Norway (or so they claimed), to visit Endewyn. They overheard Endewyn and her visitors chatting about a fanciful kingdom populated by elves, dwarves, giants, and dragons, and recalled her fondness for fairy stories.

On March 24, 2006, the last day of Endewyn's life, it was rainy, but not unpleasant. She managed to climb out of bed, shuffle to a window, and gaze over Swansea Bay one final time.

⌘

After Gaudet's hands were freed, he led them back up the stairs to the study, through the courtroom, to one of the rooms along the hall.

He opened the door with an ornate brass key. Filling the interior of the room was a bulky, tarp-covered object. Gaudet pulled the tarp off to reveal a sleek time shuttle with a bubble-shaped canopy. They all climbed inside.

Gaudet sat in the cockpit and touched some controls.

"I'm cutting the shuttle's "anchor" to this time. Sit down or grab a hold of something fast!"

The disorientation of time travel washed over Tony again. He hadn't even had time to sit.

"Steady," he heard Gaudet saying. He stumbled, recovered, and caught Caroline who was toppling next to him. Tony looked to the rear of the shuttle and saw Vanaya sitting on the floor of the cargo area with her arms around Tegwyn and Monique. Gaudet was speaking.

"LC-Veston Control, Protocol Nine, repeat Protocol Nine. Immediate jump."

Gaudet turned to the others.

"There's no time to plot out the jumps now, so we're jumping to a prearranged space/time location to cover our tracks. Hang on!"

Tony just had time to guide Caroline to a seat behind the cockpit and crouch down before being overcome by time travel vertigo and briefly blacking out.

"Where are we?" demanded Caroline angrily. She realized that she had dropped the Wolf King's lance and quickly stooped down to retrieve it. Gaudet watched her impassively, not stirring from his seat.

"A safe place, where our organization has an auxiliary control center. We're in the clear now. Once I return you people to when and where you need to be, you needn't worry about Temp Affairs people knockin' on your doors."

Tony checked to see that Vanaya and the girls were conscious, then turned back to Gaudet.

"I don't understand. Who are your controllers? Why didn't the Wolf King know you had brought us from the Time Station?"

"Ah see, as I explained to you previously, we're a private time exploration agency. I contracted out to the Wolf King to set up his operation when I thought he and his buddies were just harmless... eccentrics. When things took a turn for the uglier, I had to stay in his confidences until I found a way to nail him."

"Uh huh," said Tony, unconvinced.

"But our organization has its own control centers, and ways to cover our tracks in the time stream when necessary. I knew that your unauthorized presence on Khronos-Solarin would be eventually sniffed out by the Temps. I purposely left my temporal trail uncovered when I delivered you to the Wolf King's Temporal Proprietary so that you could be tracked back there. Because of this little adventure, I'm afraid that me and my boys are going to have to go entirely underground. Become refugees in the time stream."

Gaudet turned and looked out through the bubble canopy of the time shuttle. All that was visible was a faintly pulsing star in a sea of darkness. Tegwyn and Monique had wandered to the front of the shuttle and now stared through the canopy in wonder.

"I believe these girls have a new home to go to," said Gaudet.

After some discussion, it was decided that Vanaya and the girls would be dropped off at Luster, near the region of Norway that Vanaya had grown up in, some thirty years after the time that she had originally left. If she managed to locate any relatives, Vanaya would appear to be suitably aged for the passage of time, and explain her absence by saying that she had married and traveled overseas. The jump was made in short order, and Vanaya, Tegwyn and Monique were let off in the outskirts of the *kommune* in the early morning hours, the quaint houses, shops, and church buildings still mainly shrouded in darkness, looking for all the world like a snow globe village escaped from its glass prison and grown to full size. Caroline found tears welling in her eyes as she bade farewell to Tegwyn.

Gaudet cut anchor from early 19th Century Norway, and with the assistance of LC-Veston control jumped again to the safe space. From there, the secondary control center plotted their jump back to Corpus Christi. Gaudet's shuttle materialized in the courtyard of a deserted motel on the highway to the beach. It was exactly four hours after they had left. Tony and Caroline could see cars criss-crossing on the highway from the shuttle's cockpit and knew without a doubt that they were home at last.

"Okay Caroline, Tony. Here we are. You two stay out of trouble, hear?"

Gaudet popped open the hatch to the shuttle. The familiar humid sea-scented air flowed in.

Tony felt reluctant to leave in spite of himself. He turned back to Gaudet.

"How do we know they won't follow us here? They must know this is where we got on their time bus."

"Very true, but they won't go out of their way to find you now. It would just be more interference, and they don't like that. So unless you go out of your way to look them up..."

"We won't," said Caroline firmly.

"Oh," said Tony. "I had another question. When I first got on the time-bus, this voice said something. What was it? Something like *Passenger L, Tony Marco*. What did that mean?"

Gaudet looked genuinely puzzled. He furrowed his brow.

"Now that is something I can't explain."

"Tony!" hissed Caroline, eyeing the open hatch of the shuttle.

"Sorry Caroline, but there is one more thing I have to know. Where exactly was the Wolf King's Temporal Proprietary?"

Gaudet brightened.

"Ah, I should have known that you couldn't let that mystery remain unexplained, Tony. You see, it had to be in a place where there was a ready-made fort or castle, because the Wolf King didn't have the manpower or knowledge to build his own. It couldn't be one well known to history, because the Temps could stumble onto it on their own eventually. I must admit that discovering it is a source of personal pride to this day."

"So where...?"

"Vinland."

"Vinland?"

"So we were somewhere up in Newfoundland?"

"A bit further south than that."

"How much further south?"

"Massachusetts."

"Massachusetts?"

"Boston, to be exact."

"That was…Boston?"

"Are you up on your Colonial history, Tony? Boston was a small peninsula, practically an island connected to the mainland by a slender land bridge in days gone by. You've heard of Tremont Street? It was named after the Trimountaine, the most distinctive geographic feature of old Boston. But don't go looking for it now; the three hills were cut down in the 19th Century and used to fill in waterways around the city to create more real estate for the growing metropolis. Beacon Hill is all that remains, a shadow of its former self."

"Still, shouldn't it have been colder?"

"The climate was warmer one thousand years ago, Tony. Have you heard of the Medieval Warm Period? The Norsemen were able to maintain a colony as far north as Greenland for hundreds of years because of the milder temperatures. One of the sagas that recount the voyages to Vinland even recalls a winter without snow."

"So what happened to the Vikings who built Selwys Castle?"

"They were gone by the time the Wolf King arrived. Died off, killed, or returned to Greenland. The natives were scared off by the Wolf King's fireworks and steered clear after that."

"And kept out by the force field?"

"There was no force field. If you had strayed beyond the borders of the temporal dampening field, you would have been swooped back to your time. That's what I figured had happened to you, in fact. Seeing you sneaking about Selwys Castle was the last thing I expected."

"No force field? But the Elves told us they saw someone ripped apart by a great invisible force."

"They were swooped back to their time. To the people of Calendenny and Kevello it would have looked as if they were being seized and consumed by some terrible unknown power before their eyes."

"So if there was no force field, what kept the natives from returning?"

"Fear."

"But Paz must have known that. Why didn't she tell us?"

"Eh?"

"Never mind. But wait a minute. Someone told me that Romans had been there before the Vikings. I was sure she meant England."

"So the Romans were. Roman coins and inscriptions have been found throughout the New World, from New England to Mexico. Roman frescoes in Pompeii depict pineapple and other fruits native to the New World. And the Romans weren't even the first to visit the New World from the Old either. Now, Tony, is your mind blown?"

"Yes," he admitted.

"Now, Tony. We have to go," said Caroline impatiently, sill grasping the Wolf King's lance.

"Are you going to take that with you, Miss Caroline?" asked Gaudet.

"Actually, yes," she said.

Gaudet chuckled.

She hopped out of the shuttle.

"You stick by her side, Tony," Gaudet said.

"I plan to."

He jumped out of the hatch. "Take care, Mr. Gaudet."

Tony and Caroline turned to watch Gaudet's shuttle vanish, leaving only a dusty, litter-strewn courtyard behind them.

They walked to a nearby convenience store and borrowed a phone to call Caroline's mom. Tony mentally rehearsed a story about their phones having been stolen while they attended a Renaissance fair, but Caroline's mother didn't even ask.

"That's an interesting dress, Caroline," was the only comment she made. Caroline smirked and stretched out luxuriously in the back seat next to Tony, clutching the lance like a monarch's scepter.

Tony was dropped off in front of his house, suddenly so overwhelmed by the experience of the past several weeks that he could only mumble a quick "Bye" to Caroline. He had showered and changed into fresh clothes before his mother even noticed that he was back.

"Tony!" Elena called, knocking on his door. "Dinner's ready. Don't keep your father waiting."

"In a minute mom," he said, looking around at the walls of his room, novels in his bookcase and posters in wonder, as if seeing them for the first time. Then he turned back to his door and opened it.

"Mom!"

"What is it, son?"

"There was a story I heard once, about the time I was born. Can you remind me what happened?"

Elena blinked, caught off guard by the question.

"Why do you want to hear about that all of a sudden?"

"Just because. So I can tell my kids someday."

"We were on a family vacation on the beach. I wasn't due for a month. But I started going into labor. Your father, he absolutely panicked." She laughed at the memory.

"We went out to the parking lot, but his old Chevy wouldn't start. Then this bus driver came up to us and said he would give us a ride to the hospital. He drove a shuttle bus for tourists who stayed in local hotels. He drove like crazy, but you wouldn't wait. Your father wasn't any help, but there was another lady on board who assisted. You were born on the bus."

"On the bus," echoed Tony, as if in a trance.

"Yes. And the driver even said that he would arrange for you to get lifetime rides on their bus line. He asked me for your name, so I named you Anthony on the spot, after my uncle from Nevada."

"And then what?"

"I never heard anything after that. But it was just a little shuttle bus service, after all."

"I guess so," said Tony, smiling. Suddenly, everything felt right in the world.

"What's for dinner? Smells good."

Tony sat down at the table where his father was already piling a generous serving of Chicken Alfredo on his plate.

"Hey Dad, save some for me."

"First come, first served."

"Hey you know what? I hung out with Caroline today. We should invite her and her mom over for dinner some day."

"That would be nice," said Elena.

"Sure, why not?" added Rudy.

"Dad?"

"Yeah?"

"Could you tell me about what it was like playing in a band?"

The End

Tony and Caroline's adventures continue in Book II of *Temporal Affairs.*

Historical Notes

Chapter 8

This chapter begins with an account of a fictional landing in North America by Norse colonists from Greenland taking place approximately 1,030 A.D., loosely based upon the *Grænlendinga Saga* ("The Saga of the Greenlanders") and Eirik's Saga, accounts of Norse exploration dating from medieval times.

A Norse settlement in North America dating to roughly 1,000 A.D. was discovered at L'Anse aux Meadows in Newfoundland, Canada, in 1960 by archaeologists Anne Stine Ingstad and Helge Ingstad. The settlement at L'Anse aux Meadows is the oldest verified European colony in the New World outside of Greenland. Archaeological evidence discovered at the site suggests that L'Anse aux Meadows might have been a way station for further exploration southward into North America by Norse adventurers.

Chapter 10

The story of Estrella and Luna/Monique takes place in the Spanish city of *Jaén*, Andalucia, in 1473, the year of a violent riot or pogrom directed at Jewish *conversos* (Sephardic Jews who had been forcibly converted to Christianity). Jews were ultimately officially expelled from Spain in 1492 by the Alhambra Decree of King Ferdinand and Queen Isabella. Jewish people were allowed to live and practice their faith openly in Spain again by the 19th Century, but the Alhambra Decree was not officially revoked until December 16, 1968.

Chapter 12

Osvald Korac is Croatian, while his wife Jelena is Serbian. Croatia was one of several component nations encompassed by the Austro-Hungarian Empire until its collapse in 1918. Following World War I, Croatia joined other Slavic states, including the Kingdom of Serbia, Montenegro, Macedonia, Slovenia, and Bosnia and Herzegovina, in a union that would eventually become known as the Kingdom of Yugoslavia. After the military defeat and occupation of Yugoslavia by Germany in World War II, Croatia was controlled by the Nazi puppet state known as The Independent State of Croatia (NDH). The NDH pursued Croatian nationalist policies and persecuted Serbs, Jews, and other ethnic minorities. Following Germany's defeat, Croatia became a socialist republic within Yugoslavia. Croatia finally became an independent republic after the dissolution of Communist Yugoslavia in 1991.

Chapter 16

Gaudet finds Vendela/Vanaya II living on a small *gard* (a hereditary farming estate) in early 19th Century Norway. At that point in history, Norway had been ceded to the control of Sweden by Denmark. The prophecy of the Norse Seeress in chapter 8 is obliquely fulfilled when Vendela/Vanaya II is brought to live in Calendenny by Gaudet.

Character Time Table

1030 A.D. – The Ravenous One founds the colony at the Three Hills, begins construction of the Fort of the Three Hills.

1033 A.D. – Gaudet discovers the location of the settlement. Last of the Norsemen depart. The Wolf King arrives just as native people begin destroying the fort and outlying settlements, and begins process of re-building. He returns intermittently between 1033 A.D. and 1097 A.D., overseeing the creation of his Kingdom.

1053 A.D. – Endewyn and other genetic parents arrive at the Wolf King's Temporal Proprietary. First of the clone children are born.

1066 A.D. – Last of the original children of Calendenny and Kevello perish.

1069 A.D. – Klemens and Karlo Korac arrive at the Wolf King's Temporal Proprietary. Vendela/Vanaya II and Poppa Narvil arrive, followed by the new children of Calendenny and Kevello over the course of the next several years.

1086 A.D. – Tegwyn born.

1097 A.D. – Luna/Monique arrives at Selwys Castle. The Wolf King and his cohorts return, begin continuous habitation of Castle Selwys.

1098 A.D. – Tony and Caroline arrive at Selwys Castle, October 3. Battle of Selwys Castle takes place, November 1.

1468 A.D. – Luna/Monique born.

1473 A.D. – Gaudet rescues Luna/Monique from mob in *Jaén*, Andalucia.

1823 A.D. – Vendela/Vanaya II born.

1830 A.D. – Gaudet finds Vendela/Vanaya II in Norway.

1893 A.D. – Karlo Korac born.

1895 A.D. – Klemens Korac born.

1920 A.D. – Endewyn Celeste Vaughn born.

1931 A.D. – Karlo and Klemens accept Johannes' offer to go to Wolf King's Temporal Proprietary.

1949 A.D. – Endewyn accepts Gaudet's offer to go to Wolf King's Temporal Proprietary.

1951 A.D. – Stephen Gaudet born in Lake Charles, Louisiana.

Acknowledgements

The author wishes to acknowledge the following sources and inspirations:

The Fairy Faith in Celtic Countries, by W.Y. Evans-Wentz, 1911

The Vinland Sagas, translated by Magnus Magnusson and Hermann Palsson, Penguin Classics, 1965

"Popular Movements and Pogroms in Fifteenth-Century Castile," by Angus MacKay, *Past & Present,* Volume 55, Issue 1, May 1972

The Anderson – Amundson Family History web site, for invaluable information on Norwegian rural life and immigration to America in the 19th Century. http://freepages.genealogy.rootsweb.ancestry.com/~anderson1836/

The Lord of the Rings, by J.R.R. Tolkien, 1954-1955

The Wonderful Wizard of Oz, by L. Frank Baum, 1900

"A Sound of Thunder," by Ray Bradbury, 1952

Also, I would like to express my gratitude to my friend Karin Evans-Koleszar for her assistance and support.

www.ingramcontent.com/pod-product-compliance
Lightning Source LLC
Chambersburg PA
CBHW060056150626
46556CB00017BA/950

* 9 7 8 0 9 8 9 9 9 1 1 0 0 *